Rhiannon Cross wrote *The Dad Dilemma*, her first book, when she was only fourteen years old. Rhiannon lives in Cardiff with her two sisters, two cats, a dog and a rabbit. She is in Year Ten at school where she enjoys reading and writing but most of all she enjoys going out with her friends. She was selected by *Bliss* magazine as one of the twenty coolest teenagers of 2004.

the DAD Dilemma

100% chaos

Rhiannon Cross xxx

Piccadilly Press • London

First published in Great Britain in 2004
by Piccadilly Press Ltd.,
5 Castle Road, London NW1 8PR
Text copyright © Rhiannon Cross, 2004

A catalogue record for this book is available from the British
Library

ISBN: 1 85340 830 1 (trade paperback)

1 3 5 7 9 10 8 6 4 2

Printed and bound in Great Britain by Bookmarque Ltd
Typeset by Textype Typesetters
Cover design by Sue Hellard and Fielding Design
Set in Caslon

Thanks to everyone at Piccadilly Press for helping me achieve this, which I never thought possible. To Aimee, Alex, Alysha, Anna, Emma, Emma and Laura – the seven best friends anyone could ever wish for.
To Andrew – for making me the luckiest girl in the world. To my mum, dad, sisters Joolz and Jennie, and to everyone else who made this possible – there just isn't enough paper to mention you all.

Chapter 1

A is for the Attraction and B is for Beautiful boys

It all began one chilly morning in October. I got up, stood outside the bathroom door for twenty minutes waiting patiently for my seventeen-year-old half-sister Rachel to finish doing whatever mysterious thing she does in there. Then, after washing my hair thoroughly – to get rid of all the Plasticine and alien putty my three-year-old brother Josh had kindly put in it while I was asleep – I headed to school, singing to myself all the way.

OK, I'll admit I'm not normally that happy on my way to school, it *is* school after all. I had something dancing in my mind that morning, something that made not just my day, but my whole life, seem more worthwhile. You see, that's the effect meeting the love of your life has on you.

The day before I had been walking home from school, my big rucksack on my back packed with rubbish I didn't really need. My brown curly hair bounced with each step. I was about three minutes from my house when I saw him: the vision of loveliness, my soulmate. I was at the end of my road when he stepped off the bus. I smiled and then he winked at me.

It was so amazing, maybe the best moment of my entire life. When he looked at me, I felt this shiver tingle down my spine, like I'd turned into a big fat bowl of strawberry jelly. After he'd turned down a nearby road, gorgeous hands in his gorgeous pockets, I took a deep breath and smiled to myself. I clutched my books to my chest and spun my bag round in circles. Whoa!

Since then I hadn't been able to keep still. I felt like I had a hundred and one ants in my pants.

'Millie!' a voice called to me loudly.

That's me! Millie Addicott. Well, it's Camilla actually, but everyone I know calls me Millie.

I turned my head in the direction of the voice – definitely Patrick. He lives next door to me – well, next door to my dad – and is my best buddy. He's been my mate for as long as I can remember, though he annoys me sometimes, like when he makes fun of my height. I always used to be taller than him, but, I don't know, something happened and now he's at least half a foot taller.

He's slightly strange. He finds maths fun and hates shopping, but hey, what can you do? He's a boy, after all!

I waited as he jogged over to meet me, his light brown hair moving slightly in the wind.

'Hey, Patrick, my faithful companion. You are like sunshine on a rainy day. You are the wind beneath my wings. You are absolutely fabulous!' I said, smiling and giving him a big bear hug, almost crushing him in the process.

'What's up with you?' Patrick asked, trying to shake himself out of my grip and giving me a look which said 'get off me now or I may have to buy you a ticket to an execution, i.e., yours.'

'I'm just in a fantabulously great mood!' I said, grinning.

'Why? Did you discover you're adopted?'

'Close. Very close!'

'Well, what, then?'

'I'm in love. I've shot past the stars and am spiralling into outer space.'

'Who is it this time?' he asked in his 'I don't give a monkey's uncle about this' voice.

'I'll have you know, naive boy, that it is for real this time and to tell you the truth, I don't know his name.'

'How can you be in love with him if you don't even know his name?'

'Well, it was love at first sight and I'm sure I'll find out his name soon enough.'

'How are you going to do that?' he said, pushing his hand through his hair.

I thought for a moment, and came to the conclusion I had no idea at all.

'Well, it doesn't really matter what I call him

because as Juliet says, "What's in a name?"'

'Wow! You got it bad!' he muttered, shuffling his feet a bit.

'It is true. It is true.'

As we made our way to another day at our averagely boring school, I was so happy that I didn't even feel the chill of the October breeze on my skin. I just skipped along as Patrick trudged, not taking his eyes off the pavement.

'What's up with you, then?' I asked him, still smiling my manic wide-eyed grin. 'You look like a rainy day!'

He didn't answer at first, he just kept staring at the ground and moaning every few seconds.

'Well?' I prompted.

'It's Lucky,' he sighed, still staring at the ground like he was being followed by a huge black cloud. 'He died this morning.'

'Lucky who?' I asked. 'He obviously wasn't very lucky, was he?'

Patrick glared at me.

'Sorry, Patrick.'

Then he said in a very unhappy voice, 'He was my favourite goldfish! You know, the one with the white stripe down the side.'

I nodded. I remembered him getting that fish. About a year ago I'd gone up to his room and there it was, in a small round bowl on his desk. It was quite big for a goldfish and I remember asking him if it had enough room in there. Patrick had shrugged and said it was the biggest bowl he could afford.

He was so dedicated to that thing he would clean it out every week. I'd helped him once and we'd ended up having a water fight in the bathroom, then when his dad came in and shouted at us we were very tempted to use his toothbrush to finish cleaning the glass.

I smiled at the memory.

'That's rough,' I said, shaking my head. 'Did you bury him?'

Patrick looked at me strangely and flipped back into 'macho boy' mode.

'It was just a fish, Mill.'

I sighed. Boys really are a different species altogether.

After reaching the school gates we met up with Holly, Lucinda, Megan, Jade, Kaori and Justin. They're our mates. Well, I'm not actually that fussed about Justin. He's so distant, and it kind of scares me the way his eyes freeze behind his glasses, but he's Patrick's friend so I don't mind him being there really.

Holly's my best friend. Well, best girl friend. We've been mates since we were five.

I met her in the little house in the corner of the junior school classroom and she asked me to play with her. She looked so friendly with her big smile and bright blond hair in bunches, I just couldn't say no. She doesn't look much different now, she still has that bright blond hair, though it's shorter now, and sort of spiky.

I met the others at the beginning of secondary school.

Lucinda's just mad through and through and although sometimes she can be a lot to handle, we all love her just the way she is. Her personality definitely matches her hair. It's the most amazing bright ginger you've ever seen and it floats so wonderfully all the way down her back. She's not that fussed about it herself because quite a lot of people make fun of her for it. I don't know what they're on about, I think it's gorgeous.

Megan's the quiet one, but then again she's not *that* quiet. She's just shy around people she doesn't know. With us, she's a different person. She used to have really long brown hair; it was dead straight and so shiny. Then one day, she came into school with it cut to her shoulders and has worn it like that ever since. Her eyes match her hair – really strong brown.

Jade is so clever, she makes us all feel a bit on the stupid side sometimes. It's not like she's good at one or two things, she's good at everything. It just doesn't seem fair. She has short black hair, feathered at the front which looks totally gorgeous with her amazing cheekbones.

Kaori's reasonably new to the school. She came at the beginning of the year. She said our group looked the friendliest. That was sweet of her, though maybe everyone else had just told her to bog off.

'Hey, Millie!' Kaori said with a smile. 'You'll never guess what happened.'

I sighed. Kaori always seemed to have news. I wanted to tell everyone about my soulmate.

'I won that gymnastics competition, you know, the one I've been training for since like, for ever!'

No surprise there, I thought. It's unbelievable how many gymnastics trophies Kaori has. The whole of her living room is just bursting with them. And everyone knows she's the best in the world at it. Not to mention she looks like she stepped out of *Vogue* because she was just too beautiful to hang around there any more. With her beautiful silky black hair and dark chocolate skin, she really is stunning.

'That's great, Kaz, and guess what . . .' I started to say.

But everyone gathered round Kaori and started congratulating her, like it was some huge surprise.

'Well done, Kaori!'

'You must have been fab!'

'I can't believe it!'

'Listen!' I yelled.

Everyone turned to look at me.

'I have some news too! You see, I met the most gorgeous boy on the way home from school yesterday!'

Everybody looked at me for all of two seconds and then turned right back around and continued with what they were saying.

'Can you teach me a few moves?'

'Did you do your front flip thing?'

Why doesn't anyone care about me? I thought as I stared at the crowd of friends all discussing Kaori's latest triumph.

'Hey, Mill!' Jade said turning to look at me at last. 'Who's your latest crush, then? Anyone we know?'

'He's not just a crush, Jade!' I sighed, staring at the clouds.

'He's her One True Love,' Patrick pointed out sarcastically. I started to glare at him in my 'you insensitive loser' way, but after I'd seen the stubborn look on his face I decided to stop myself. He looked like he was in a pretty bad mood – surely it wasn't just the goldfish.

'What's his name, then? This *gorgeous* bloke?' Lucinda asked, her wavy ginger hair blowing slightly across her face.

'He doesn't have one!' Patrick said.

'Does so!' I replied, sneering.

'What is it, then?' Patrick taunted.

'Well,' I said, turning to the others, 'I don't actually know it. I haven't had a chance to speak to him yet!'

Holly, Jade, Megan, Kaori and Lucinda all sniggered. Patrick stared at me. God knows what Justin was doing, he seemed to be staring into the sky.

'What?' I exclaimed at everyone's giggle outbreak.

Nobody said a word. All I could hear was soft sniggering and the faint sound of chewing from Patrick's open mouth.

Chapter 2

C is for Cold and
D is for 'Don't scare me!'

It was chilly again on Saturday morning and I was strolling down my quiet road with Patrick. We were on our way to the park to meet the others, something we did every weekend. Though sadly, with the weather getting worse every day, it seemed like we'd have to change our meeting place (i.e., to somewhere indoors) pretty soon.

'So,' Patrick said, 'do you still have the hots for umm . . . thingamabob?'

I smiled at him. 'Absolutely! You don't just stop fancying the pants off a guy like that!'

'I think it's silly!' he muttered.

'What's silly?' I asked him as I popped another chocolate button into my open mouth and chewed contentedly.

'Fancying someone you don't even know!'

'Don't you believe in love at first sight?'

'Yes . . . no . . . I dunno. It's just this is the third guy this month you've fallen in love with at first sight.'

I sighed. 'This time it's totally different!'

'How?'

'It just feels different. Like I could do anything!'

'Well, chuck yourself off a high building, then, maybe you'll fly!'

'Patrick! What's up with you? Aren't you happy for me?'

'Well, just don't rush into anything. You're my mate and I care about you a lot.'

I reached right over and hugged him. 'And I care about you too, mate! Hey, do you want to go out somewhere Thursday night?'

'I thought you were going out with your dad?'

I shuffled my feet, thinking, Yeah, me too. I planned to go out to dinner with my dad, because we always did. Every Thursday at seven o'clock he picked me up from my mum's and we went out to eat somewhere. He always treated me to an amazing meal, with (most importantly) an absolutely *huge* dessert. But this time he'd rung up and decided to cancel . . . again!

'Umm . . . he had to cancel.'

'Again? Didn't he cancel last time? And a few weeks ago? And . . .'

'Yes, yes, he did, all right!'

'Why?'

'I don't know why!' I snapped.

Patrick looked at me, shocked and surprised.

'I'm sorry, Pat, I didn't mean to bite your head off!'

'It's OK, no worries!' he said, smiling in his own friendly way.

'Anyway, I'm not *that* bothered,' I lied. 'I'm still going to see him this afternoon, and I get to stay until Monday. So I don't mind that much, it's not a big deal.'

Patrick raised his eyebrows like he didn't quite believe me. I smiled at him and turned away, so he couldn't see the small tear threatening to trickle down from my eye.

Patrick and I entered the park and headed over to meet Kaori and Jade. Unfortunately, Kaori had to bring her annoying boyfriend, Danny, along. He's in a rock band at our school and thinks he is incredibly handsome, which is true, but he doesn't have to flaunt it, does he? She's been going out with him for about a month now and I can't stand it when she's with him, because she turns into a complete bimbo, when really she's as smart as anything.

But he is the boyfriend of one of my best mates and I had to accept that the self-obsessed, completely and utterly boring loser would be coming along. I mean, the worst thing about him is this look he gives you – it makes you feel so insignificant and that you're not worth being alive. He acts all sweet and normal with Kaori, but can't she see beyond the front he puts on for her?

I couldn't see the rest of the gang anywhere and wished Holly had changed her mind about coming. I knew where she was – well, not exactly, but yesterday she had been moaning about how childish it was to meet your mates down at the park and why couldn't we all get cool boyfriends and go out to cool places together.

Well, the first reason being we actually *like* hanging out in the park and the second being that we'd actually have to get boyfriends which is difficult when everyone in the school knows you as the Swot Gang. We're not swots, it's only because we don't smoke or skip maths at every opportunity.

It's OK for Kaori, even though she's in our 'swot gang' and is as clever as anything, her looks and confidence seem to cancel all of this out. She's so confident about everything and I suppose that's why all the boys like her.

'Hi!' I said cheerily. 'No Holly?'

Jade shrugged and Kaori was too busy kissing Danny to answer me.

'Oh well, guess it's just us, then!'

Kaori unstuck her lips and smiled at me.

It was Danny who had the clever idea of us all playing hide and seek in South Gate Wood. Little did I know this would reveal something that had maybe already been there, but I'd never noticed.

I was strolling through the wood by myself. The trees were so close together they blocked out most of the sunlight. I was starting to pick an obvious hiding place so I'd be found quickly and wouldn't have to stay in the depths of the forest alone for too long, when I heard a rustling that I didn't quite like behind a nearby bush.

Don't be paranoid, I told myself. It's just some kind of woodland creature moving around.

I started to think about my dad to distract myself. Why couldn't he be bothered with me any more? What had changed? He used to love spending time with me, and, although sometimes I wasn't crazy about going places with him, I suppose I missed them now that we didn't go any more.

At least I was going to his house when I was done at the park. I was meant to be there about half-past twelve. What time is it now? I wondered, looking at my bare wrist and remembering the purple watch sitting on the table in my room. I couldn't have long left.

My thoughts didn't distract me from the rustling bush for very long, however. It was all I could hear and without thinking I found myself tiptoeing and making very little noise, so whatever was rustling wouldn't hear me.

Just go and check it out, I thought. Once you see that there's nothing there, then you'll feel better.

After a couple of minutes of anxious waiting by a large tree I decided to find the source of the noise. Then maybe I could stop shaking with fear and get on with the hiding.

I slowly crept up to the bush that was doing all the

swishing and swashing, trying to make as little noise as I could, because if it was a mad psychopath waiting for fresh teenager, I didn't want him to hear me. I stopped a few short steps away from the psychopathic bush to contemplate my next move.

'Boo!'

I shrieked and jumped fifty feet in the air.

'You should have seen your face!' Patrick exclaimed, laughing. 'You were so scared.'

Once I caught my breath again, I gave him one of my 'you're in trouble' looks. He was still laughing uncontrollably like a hyena with a very bad sense of humour.

'That was a very sick joke, Patrick!' I said, still gasping. 'I thought you were some sort of serial murderer.'

More giggling.

'You could have given me a heart attack!'

More giggling.

'You could have flipping killed me!'

More giggling.

I stopped speaking and started to walk off. The thought of hanging out with a manic Patrick wasn't really very appealing. Though neither was going back into the scary woods alone.

'I'll stay here,' I decided out loud.

Patrick stopped giggling for a second to say, 'Oh! Is poor Millie scared of the bogeyman?'

He burst out laughing again.

Once Patrick had stopped his wild laughing fit, we headed off in search of the others.

'Whose stupid idea was this anyway?' I said sulkily.

'Danny's, of course!' Patrick sighed, looking at me with a twinkle in his eye that I didn't know quite how to interpret. 'But I bet he found Kaori first and they're deeply involved in a snogging fest right now.'

I grunted, trying to act cool and look as though I wasn't still shaking. I'll admit that even with Patrick there, I was still the teeniest bit afraid. I'd rather be eating one of DM's fry-ups than standing in a dark forest alone with Patrick, I thought. (DM is my mum's annoying boyfriend and father to my irritating three-year-old brother Josh. His fry-ups are not a joyful experience.)

'Where *are* they?' I asked, wrapping my arms around myself. 'It's getting cold!'

'Here!' Patrick said, smiling and offering me his blue fleece. 'Take this!'

I raised one eyebrow at him, wondering why he was being so nice all of a sudden. He popped his jacket over my arms and when his hand touched mine, I got this all-over tingly feeling, like some kind of electric current spreading through my skin.

Patrick stared at me, and I stared back.

'Millie? Patrick? Is that you?' We heard Kaori's faraway voice call.

I snapped out of whatever state I was in. Was I blushing?

'Hey, we've been looking for you for positively

ages!' Jade sighed, giving me an odd look. 'Why are you wearing Patrick's fleece?'

I looked down at the fleece and then back at her. 'I was cold.'

'Have you seen Danny?' Kaori asked. 'I have to be going and I don't want to leave without saying goodbye.'

'I think you mean snogging goodbye.' I said, smiling.

Kaori gave me a thump on the arm and shook her head. 'Oi, you!'

'I think we should all be heading off. What time is it anyway?'

Kaori lifted her right arm into the light and squinted. 'Half one.'

'Oh no!' I cried, creating an echoey din through the forest. 'I was meant to be at my father's by now!'

I quickly removed Patrick's fleece and thrust it in his direction, then ran off at high speed (which isn't that high, with little legs), trying not to be too freaked out by the general eeriness of the woods around me.

Chapter 3

E is for Everything turning upside down and F is for Finding out the truth

I visit my dad every Saturday. At half-past twelve I take the bus up to his house, which is about a twenty-minute walk from my mum's and spend the weekend with him.

Although we used to go places after school on Thursdays; out to dinner, to the cinema, out shopping or something else, I haven't done anything like that with him for ages. He always seems to cancel, and although I wouldn't say I treasure every moment with my dad (he's an annoying old man most of the time) it still hurts when he calls it off. It's like he's so busy that he just can't find the time to see his only daughter any more.

The absolute worst thing is that he doesn't bother to give me a reason at all. It's like some kind of big secret that he won't let me in on! Every time it's, 'Oh, I can't make it tomorrow. Something really important has come up. Maybe next time,' though the next time it's the same, and the next and the next! It seems like he has the time to do lots of things, just not to see me.

Has he decided to take up fencing, or something?

Anyway, I caught the bus up to his house, using up the last of this week's pocket money. I was almost two hours late when I eventually arrived at the door. I could hear Mr Goggle's bark two streets away. He's our terrorising terrier and for a dog the size of a small cat, he can sure let off a lot of noise.

I opened the door, only to be slobbered on from head to foot by Mr Goggle (well, from foot to knee actually).

'Millie?' I heard my dad call from the kitchen in his rampaging father voice. 'Where the hell have you been?'

I wiped myself free of doggy drool and tried to slip quietly upstairs, only Mr Goggle had left his squeaky toy newspaper in the middle of my path and it let out a huge tell-tale squeal.

'Where do you think you're going?' my dad yelled as his bald head came into view.

I sighed and looked around the messy hallway. Some inconsiderate person (mentioning no names, Dad) had left my history project on the floor with a wonderful coffee stain in the centre. Well, I suppose the coffee stain was Dad's fault and Mr Goggle was to blame for stealing it and leaving it in the hall. Who knew he had a taste for Hitler? It had taken me hours to finish and was due in next week. Now I was going to have to do parts again. If only I hadn't left it on the kitchen table where people could rest their mugs on it.

The bookshelf was overflowing with anything but books (like a three-day-old half-drunk cup of hot chocolate). The phone was covered in sticky fingerprints, which I knew must be down to Alison, the five-year-old next-door neighbour who hangs out in our house all the time (could be something to do with the fact that her mum fancies Dad in a big way). The pictures that were once neat and pristine in their frames were coated in a layer of dust so thick it was quite a challenge to see the picture at all. Welcome home! I thought, staring at the frown on Dad's face and then at the mangled project that was now hanging out of Mr Goggle's mouth. Welcome home indeed!

I suppose I should be used to the mess by now, but somehow it still takes me by surprise when I walk through the door.

'I've been trying to call you. Why didn't you have your phone on?'

I shrugged. 'I left it here last week, it's in my room.'

'So, why are you late?'

'I'm sorry, I just lost track of time.'

He wiggled his head around in three hundred and twenty-two circles and let out a huge groan meaning, I don't have time for this.

'Look,' he started, rubbing his running nose on his blue sleeve. 'I'll be lenient with you just this once, though that's only because we have a guest!'

This puzzled me. A guest? Who in this universe (apart from Alison, the mental girl, and her lovesick

19

mother) would be insane enough to visit this hellhole out of their own free will?

'Who?' I asked.

'You'll see!' he smiled in a cunning and very abnormal way. 'I'll bring her through now!'

Her? Since when has Dad been entertaining women in his house? Since the Twelfth of Never, that's when. I mean, he can hardly be considered attractive. He may have been once, though it's hard to tell. His wrinkles have taken over his entire face and his hair is in such small proportions that unless you carry a mini microscope around in your handbag, you wouldn't even know it existed at all.

Anyway, after fighting for his trouser leg with Mr Goggle, Dad disappeared into the kitchen leaving me by the front door holding my mangled project in one hand and Mr Goggle's squeaky newspaper in the other. There was an extremely puzzled expression currently inhabiting my face.

My dad emerged wearing a silly grin that confused me for more than a moment.

'I'd like you to meet my new girlfriend Abby!'

New girlfriend? What did he mean, new girlfriend? New as opposed to old? Meaning, he's had one before? Since when? Why hadn't he told me?

He stepped aside to reveal a blonde woman about the same size as him, maybe slightly smaller, who must have been in her early thirties. Much too young for my dad!

'But . . .' I stuttered. 'You've never been out with anyone before. You're too old!'

My dad threw his head back and let out a roar of laughter. 'You're never too old for love, Mill!'

'Nice to meet you!' Abby smiled, holding out her hand for me to shake.

I stretched my hand out towards hers and shook it reluctantly. Her hands were smooth, but in a 'too much hand cream' kind of way. I didn't like them, I didn't like her. How could my dad have a girlfriend? It was insane!

'Abby's an artist!' my dad said, beaming at me. 'She owns the art shop down in the village. You know, we used to go there when you were little. It's a small world, isn't it?'

He turned to Abby and gave her a goofy smile. Their lips met and Abby let out a tiny giggle. I stared in horror.

'Hey, Millie, Abby has some of her work through here. It really is very good, I thought you might like to take a look.'

'Umm . . . I'd love to, but umm . . . I have some homework to do!' I sighed. 'It's very important!'

I ran up the stairs and lay on my bed for a few minutes sucking an old lollypop that I'd just found on my desk. Mr Goggle had followed me up, but after I had shut the door in his face, he seemed to get the message. My room wasn't the most relaxing of places, the fact that it had no wallpaper didn't really help. (Dad had had a mad DIY phase and stripped it all off, but after he'd got going, he decided it wasn't really his scene after all.)

So that was why he'd been cancelling our meetings! Did he really want to spend more time with her than with me?

I took several deep breaths, had a good cry and then played with my teddies for a while. I'd been up there about twenty minutes when the broken door suddenly began to shake and make a tap-tapping noise.

'Can I come in?' I heard my dad call.

'I guess . . .'

He opened the door and then closed it behind him.

'Are you OK with this situation?' he asked me with a look of true concern in his eyes. 'Because Abby doesn't have to stay. I'll ask her to leave if you like.'

'No, Dad! It's fine – honestly!'

'Then why are you avoiding eye contact?'

I sighed and turned to look at his sorry face, hoping that all traces of tears were gone. He didn't say anything so I assumed I was safe.

'I can't control your life, Dad. You *have* been divorced a while now!'

He smiled. 'Good, just as long as it's OK with you.'

He left the room, leaving me alone to drown myself in salty tears.

I sat up for a moment and gazed around the room until the tears from my eyes dried away and I could see again. Then I picked up my pink mobile phone from the desk and scrolled through the list of numbers, carefully deliberating over who to call. I mean, I had to call someone. I needed to hear a friendly, caring voice at the other end of the phone, but who to call – now that was tricky.

Normally, I wouldn't have to think about it at all. I would just call Patrick. He's my best friend and I tell him everything before anyone else. But just then, somehow I didn't feel I could talk to him. I was feeling really confused about what happened in the woods. What was that feeling earlier? Did it mean something? Why had this suddenly happened? I'd never had anything like that happen before. This was Patrick, my best friend, someone I *definitely* wasn't attracted to. What about the dream boy who stepped off the bus? Surely he was my soulmate? I just had to find him again and all would be right.

In the end I decided to call Holly. She's my best girl friend, after all. I mean, sometimes she can annoy me like crazy, bitching about people, telling me my hair looks like a wild jungle, but I see she's only being honest. She's only saying out loud what everyone else is thinking and I suppose I admire her for that. It's just I've known her so long and we know everything there is to know about each other. She always seems to help me out too.

'Hey Holly, you'll never guess what just happened.'

'What? Is it exciting?' she almost giggled, in an interested sort of way.

I shook my head, and then realised I was on the phone and she couldn't see so I muttered, 'Not really, it's just worrying!'

'Well, what's happened, then?'

I took a deep breath and had a quick check that Dad and the 'artistic genius' weren't around. Then I muttered, 'My dad's only gone and got himself a girlfriend.'

'Really? What insane woman would go out with your dad?' she asked cheekily.

'Oi!'

'Sorry, just kidding!'

'So what should I do about it?'

'About what?' she asked, puzzled.

'My dad's girlfriend, of course!'

'I don't see the problem.'

I sighed. Holly is so naive sometimes.

'I need to get rid of her!'

'Why?'

'Because she's a bitch!'

'You only just met her. How do you know she's a bitch?'

I sighed. 'She just is, OK? So please help me get rid of her!'

'No, Millie! I don't really think you should get involved!'

'But . . .'

'No means no!'

'Holly, why do you always have to be so horrible?'

'Bye, Mill!'

And with that her phone was back on the hook. Just for once, couldn't she try to see it from my point of view?

Chapter 4

G is for Going slowly insane

I flicked back through the names in my phone and hit Holly's call button again. She hung up on me. I tried again with the same result. Maybe Holly's 'tell everyone exactly what I think' quality wasn't always a good thing. I sighed to myself. I wasn't going to leave it like that. I can't stand arguing with Holly, it takes over my mind and I can't think of anything else! And I need to keep my mind as clear as possible at the moment. So I glanced out of the window and studied the weather outside. It looked cold, but it was still sunny. I thundered down the stairs, grabbed my coat from the hook and ran out of the door.

'Going to Holly's, Dad!' I yelled as I shut the door behind me.

It wasn't actually that cold outside and with my coat on, I really didn't feel it at all. Anyway, my mind was using all its energy, chugging away trying to think of what I was going to say to Holly when I had finished trudging the half-hour walk to her house.

What could I say to her that would make her understand?

I kicked through the fallen leaves and listened as they swished and crackled underfoot. It didn't help my thinking, but it did help my frustration. I kicked them harder. 'Stupid Abby! Stupid Dad!'

It was then that I realised it was after three o'clock and I hadn't eaten anything for lunch. I hadn't been hungry up to this point, but the thought of food made my tummy grumble. No. No food, not just yet!

When I finally reached Holly's I stopped outside the front gate. Why was I there? Holly's family were, well, they were OK, but I wasn't really in the mood to deal with them right now.

Anyway, that didn't matter, I was here to patch things up with Holly, and it was my fault after all.

I rang the doorbell and stood on the step, waiting for a reply.

'Oh,' Holly said when she opened the door, 'it's you!'

'Yeah, umm . . . I couldn't come in, could I?'

She nodded reluctantly and stepped aside to let me in. We stood in the hall for a moment, in a silence so thick you could have cut it with a knife.

'Well?' she sighed rather impatiently.

'Can we go upstairs?'

'I guess.'

So I kicked my shoes off and followed her up to her room. Once there, we sat on the bed, just looking at each other. I was waiting for her to say something and she was waiting for me.

'Look, I'm really sorry, Holly, you know, for saying you were horrible and for sounding like such a spoilt brat. I mean, I was just totally shocked, it was something I really wasn't expecting!'

Holly twiddled her fingers and played with the duvet on her bed. She sighed and lifted her eyes to look at me.

'Millie, I've known you . . . well . . . I've known you for ever and I . . . well . . . I've never known you to *ever* sound like a spoilt brat OK? I know you didn't mean to sound selfish or anything. I know that's not you.'

'So, why did you hang up on me?'

'I hung up on you because I knew what would happen if I didn't! You have a way of convincing me to do things, Mill! Even when I don't think it's the right thing to do. Ever since we were little, you could always get me to do anything. I didn't want to get involved and I knew that if I let you talk to me about it any more, you'd convince me to do it. I just knew!'

She took a deep breath and sighed loudly.

'And I know that in a few minutes I'll be agreeing to help you out. Why did you have to come around here, Mill? I would really rather not get involved.'

'I know you would!' I said, smiling and reaching over to hug her. 'But I'm not just going to sit here and watch Abby take my dad away from me! He's already cancelled everything in the last few weeks. It's her, I know it is. I just know! And I'm not going to sit around, watching her take him away, OK? You understand that, right?'

She nodded. 'I guess I can see where you're coming from. I don't know what I'd do if my dad started to spend a lot less time with me. I'd probably be just as shocked and upset as you are now.'

'I'll go now, OK? But I'll text you later, yeah?'

'Yeah. See you!'

The walk back seemed to be over in no time at all. My mind was ticking over with ideas to remove Abby from my life. I just couldn't see a way to pull any of them off.

Once home, I had a nasty shock. Well, I won't say it was a complete surprise, but I walked in on my dad and Abby kissing the mouths off each other.

'Oh . . . I'm sorry, Millie!' my dad apologised, unsticking himself from Abby's luminous red lipstick-covered lips. 'Sorry!'

I groaned a loud groan that might have resembled that of an overweight rhinoceros, before trudging back upstairs to the sanctuary of my own room. I stayed there until I heard my dad call, 'Millie! Your pizza's ready!'

That got me heading down the half-carpeted stairs pretty skittish, but after seeing the mangled burnt pizza and the gooey happy couple, I suddenly lost my appetite for pizza and for life!

Why couldn't my dad just get a goldfish? They're so much easier to deal with.

On Monday morning (after unwanted licking all over from Mr Goggle), I headed downstairs for breakfast. Abby was sitting at the table eating a bowl of Dad's favourite muesli. The muesli he won't let anyone touch, not even me, and she was eating it!!! And, to make matters worse, she was eating it while wearing Dad's dressing gown. I tried very hard to hide my disgust.

She smiled. 'Hello, Camilla! Lovely morning, isn't it?'

I winced at the sound of my full name – I really can't stand it – and stared out of the french windows at the cold misty garden outside.

'Umm . . . yeah,' I sighed. 'Amazing.'

She smiled at me again and put another spoonful of muesli into her mouth.

'How's my snuggle-bunny today, then?' My father said, smiling at Abby as he entered the room.

'Perfect,' she said, giggling as Dad kissed her neck.

'Do you want a lift to school today, pumpkin?' my dad asked, grinning at me.

I was totally shocked. Dad never offered to give me a lift. Maybe he was going to start paying more attention to me. Maybe things were about to change for the better. Maybe I wouldn't have to get rid of Abby at all.

'Cause if you want, Abby can drive you.'

Maybe . . . not.

I shook my head and muttered, 'I'm walking with Patrick.'

He nodded. 'Well, I had best be off, then.' He kissed Abby again and tossed a half-smile in my direction. 'I'll be seeing you two lovely ladies later!'

Because I stay with my dad every Saturday to Monday, I'm always heading to school from his on Monday mornings. I always wait outside Patrick's house next door for him to come out and then we walk the small ten-minute route to school together. This morning Patrick failed to arrive, though.

I waited a few minutes longer than usual, standing in the drizzle, willing him to come out of his house. In the end I had to resort to ringing the doorbell. There was no answer and so in the end I had to move on. Where was he? Why didn't he call to say he wasn't walking with me? Was he ill?

At school I engaged myself in the usual boring conversations about hair, make-up and boys, the usual chatter of Holly and Lucinda while the rest of us stand and pretend to listen. The two of them are just so talkative. I suppose that's why they disagree a lot. They have the strongest opinions.

I couldn't help but wonder where Patrick was. Why hadn't he dropped by, or even just called to say he wouldn't be coming? Was he avoiding me? What if he had been knocked over by a bus and was in hospital, fighting for his life? No, no, that couldn't be it!

Could it?

I reluctantly went back to my dad's after school on Monday. I wasn't looking forward to another night there. Dad seemed happy I was there, but in my mind I found myself wondering why. Did he want to show me he did still want to spend time with me even though he had another woman in his life? Or did he simply hope if I spent more time with Abby, I would grow to like her quicker?

I was lying on my bed, listening to some catchy tune on the radio when my dad knocked the door.

'Phone for you, Millie!'

'Who is it?'

'Umm . . . I dunno. A boy?'

I snatched the phone off him and mumbled into the crackling receiver.

'Hello?'

'Hi, Mill, it's me!' a rather croaky voice said from the other end.

'Patrick!' I practically yelled. 'Where the hell have you been?'

It was at this point I realised that my nosy father was still standing at the door, listening in. I tried to push him out. He resisted.

'For God's sake, can't I just have a phone conversation in peace?'

He rolled his eyes and disappeared down the stairs.

'Sorry,' I said back into the phone, 'eavesdropping father!'

'Well,' Patrick croaked, 'I have a really bad cold. I think I died already.'

'Aaww, poor you. But you weren't at your house. I was standing in the cold for fifteen minutes waiting for you this morning!'

'I had to go to the doctor with my mum. She's such a fusspot, I tried to tell her it was just a cold, but would she listen?'

'You could've called, couldn't you?'

There was a small space of hesitation before he replied.

'Well, my mum wouldn't let me use the phone. She probably thinks that using the phone when you're ill passes the germs down to the person at the other end.'

'How come you're calling now, then?'

'She's out at the shops. I don't have long, mind!'

Something in his voice made me forgive him instantly and I smiled to myself.

'Well, you'll never guess what happened!'

'You're going to Mars next week?'

'Umm . . . no.'

'You've grown an extra leg?'

'Umm . . . no!'

'Holly's decided to get her tongue pierced?'

'No!'

'You're . . .'

'Patrick! Stop guessing!'

'There's . . . oh, sorry. Carry on.'

'Well, my dad's got a girlfriend!'

'Really?'

'Yes.'

'Wow! I guess that's why he's been cancelling so much later. That bites big time!'

'Really? You understand? Everyone else says it's great news and that I should be happy. Then I feel really stupid for hating her!'

'You're not stupid! Of course you're not!'

'Well, will you help me, then?' I asked.

'What do you want help with?'

'I need to get rid of her!'

'Like how?'

'I don't know! I just know I have to do it, and I have to do it soon!'

'Umm . . . OK, sure. I'll help you!'

'Great!' I said. 'Thank you! Have you got any ideas to start with?'

'Umm . . .'

I walked across the room and flopped back on to my bed, listening to the breathing at the other end, Patrick's breathing. This was strangely comforting, to know that he was there, at the other end of the phone.

'Well, you could just be really well . . . be really horrible to her, be sulky and moody and make her miserable.'

'Will that do anything at all?'

'Of course it will! Adults hate moaning kids.'

'OK then, I'll activate operation Moody Teen right away!'

'Good on you, Agent C!'

I giggled. 'Talk to you tomorrow, Agent P!'

I hit the 'end call' button and listened as the droning dial tone came back to life.

'Millie, your tea's ready!' I heard my dad call from the kitchen.

I smiled. It was time to put the plan into action!

Abby smiled in my direction. 'Camilla, could you pass the salad, please?'

I stared at my plate and continued to twirl the mashed potato round with the fork. I said nothing.

'Camilla?' she asked, still smiling.

I watched the potato fall from the fork and back on to the plate. I still said nothing.

'Millie!' my dad said. 'Didn't you hear? Pass the salad to Abby, please!'

I sighed loudly and lifted my eyes from my plate. I looked at my dad, with his creased eyebrows and boring shirt.

'Pass the salad please, Millie!' he repeated.

I stretched my arms across the table, grasped the

salad bowl and moved it in the direction of Abby's plate. I didn't remove the scowl on my face. My dad noticed.

'Something wrong, Mill?'

'Umm . . . no,' I mumbled. 'Just . . . swallowed a pea.'

Chapter 5

H is for Hunger and I is for I can do this!

The next morning I woke up to the sound of my mobile ringing. I groaned, wiped my eyes and glanced at the clock. It was seven in the morning. Only one person would call at this time – my sister! She's a seventeen-year-old drama queen, completely obsessed with her looks. Thank goodness I'm only half-related to her, I suppose she must get the whole 'vain' thing from her father's side.

'Hello?' I grumbled into the phone.

'Hiya, Mill!' Rachel said cheerily. 'Good morning!'

I climbed out of bed and started to pull my trousers on.

'Hi Rach, umm . . . why are you calling me?'

'Ah, no reason. I was just doing my nails and I thought I'd call someone.'

'Oh, umm . . . OK.'

'And I thought, who can I call? Who'll be up at this time? And I thought of you.'

I dabbed some water on my eyes, feeling myself wake up slightly.

'Oh, right.'

'Anyhoo . . . I did it, Mill! I really did it!'

'What did you do?'

'IT!'

'Umm . . . what?'

'What do you mean "what"? Only the thing I've been worrying about doing for simply *ages*!'

'Sorry Rach, you'll have to tell, it's too early for guessing games.'

I heard a long sigh, followed by, 'I finally asked him out!'

'Who? Harris?'

'Yeah! Isn't that great! You are now talking to the girlfriend of *the* most gorgeous guy in the entire world!'

I sighed. Harris is nothing compared to Dream Boy, I thought to myself.

'Well, do *you* have any news?'

'Umm . . .' I scanned my brain for a moment and thought hard. 'My dad has a girlfriend.'

'Oh wow, that is *such* amazing news! Pinch me!'

'Shut up, Rach! Anyway, I doubt she'll be around long!'

'What you mean?'

'I'm hoping to get rid of her.'

'Ohmygod, Mill! You're not serious, are you?'

'Yes, very serious!'

'That is, like, so immature! I mean, could you get any more spoilt and silly? Deal with it, Mill. Love happens!'

'Immature?'

'Yes! Oh drat, I've smudged my nail polish. I have to go. Bye, Mill!'

I glanced back to the phone in my hand and shook my head. I still hadn't woken up properly. How could Rachel have called me immature? She was the one getting madly excited about a stupid boy who wasn't even *that* good-looking. (Dream Boy! Dream Boy! Dream Boy!!!)

Anyway, I wasn't being silly and immature, was I? I wasn't being selfish. It was Abby who was the selfish one. It was definitely not like my dad to cancel, but then she came along and that's all he ever seemed to do. She was *always* around. Didn't she have a home of her own? Couldn't she respect my time with my father?

She was taking him away from me.

I gathered my things together and headed out the door. I wandered up the road to see Patrick standing at the bus stop, his huge grin aimed right at me.

'Hey!' I smiled. 'You got out today, then?'

'Yes, I did indeed!'

'You don't look too bad.'

'I know. Must have been a twenty-four-hour thing or something!'

We headed down the same old road chatting about something or other. I just watched him as he talked. The way his lip curved when he said the word 'every'.

I wondered what it would be like to kiss those lips.

Where had *that* come from? I shook my head in an attempt to get that thought out of it.

'Hey, did you start on the plan, then?'

'Umm . . . well sort of. Abby asked me to pass her the salad and I ignored her.'

'And?'

'And then my dad asked me to pass it. I ignored him too, but then he got angry and asked me again and I gave in.'

'So you passed it?'

'Yes!'

'Oh, that plan's not going to work, then.'

'How do you mean?'

'If you can't even keep hold of the salad, how are you meant to move on to stage two? How can you hold, say, the potatoes?'

I watched him as his face broke out into a huge grin. Then he started laughing like crazy!

Then, despite myself, I started to giggle. 'Shut up!'

He kept laughing.

'Shut up!'

The laughing didn't stop.

'Shut up!' I laughed as I jumped on his back.

'Get off!' he said, shaking himself loose.

He grabbed my shoulders and looked into my eyes. We both fell silent. His face lowered, moving closer to mine. I panicked and pulled away.

'Oh look, we're almost at school!' I stuttered.

'Oh, um . . . yeah!' he said uneasily. 'We'd better hurry, we don't want to be late.'

That night I returned to my mum's house. I'd never been so happy to be there, it was so clean and orderly. It was great, watching my mum cook the dinner, Josh jumping up and down on the sofa, DM reading the newspaper and Rachel painting her nails, again and again.

I went up to my room and lay on my bed and stared at the twirling pattern on the ceiling. I could hear my mum and DM giggling downstairs. My sister was locked in her purple room next door, playing some rock band on top volume, and my little brother was really hyper. He'd just come back from a friend's birthday party, where he'd eaten *a lot* of cake.

I was still thinking about this morning. Had Patrick been about to kiss me? Or was that just my vivid imagination taking control? I was so confused.

I jumped at the sound of the phone ringing. I waited for my mum to answer, but after the third ring I gave in, and stretched my hand across to the phone.

'Hello?'

'Hi, Millie! It's umm . . . me.'

'Hi, Kaori! What's up?'

'It's . . . it's . . .' The voice at the other end broke out into a series of furious sobs. 'It's my dad! He's . . . he's . . . he's having an affair!'

'Oh,' I said, shocked and surprised. I had absolutely no idea what to say. 'Really?'

'No! He's not really! I'm just making this all up for attention!' she shouted. 'Of course *really*, Mill!'

'Sorry! I meant, are you totally sure?'

'Yes! I am!'

'Well, how did you find out?'

'I saw him!'

I waited for her to continue and when she said nothing, I asked, 'You saw him where?'

'With *her*! I was sitting in the living room, and a car pulled up outside. It was a red sports car. There was a woman with brown hair driving it, and . . . and my dad was in the passenger seat.'

'Oh,' I sighed. 'That's awful.'

'What do I do, Mill?'

'Umm . . . I don't know, Kaz. I really don't.'

There was another outbreak of tears. I listened as the crying got louder and louder.

'Please. You have to help. Oh, I have to go! He's coming up here. Please don't tell anyone.'

'I won't.'

'Bye!'

The phone went dead and the dial tone rang fresh in my ears. What a mess! Poor Kaori! But I had no idea what she wanted me to do about it. If I couldn't even solve my own dad dilemma, how could I solve hers?

* * *

'Millie,' my mum said as she opened the bedroom door, 'I was wondering if you could watch Josh for a bit.'

'Umm . . . why?' I asked.

'I've just realised that I'm missing mushrooms, so I'm going to have to pop out to the shops. Max has disappeared as usual.'

I smiled. 'Sure, no problem! How long will you be?'

A crease formed over her eyebrows. It's the sign of her thinking.

'I'm not too sure. I shouldn't more than half an hour, but who knows what the queues will be like.'

I nodded while quickly grabbing my diary. Josh was getting dangerously near. He'd crept into the room while Mum was holding the door open.

'Josh, put that down!' I yelled as the little boy furiously shook my jewellery box up and down. He shook it once more and dropped it.

Mum gave me a look to say sorry.

'It's OK,' I said, smiling. 'I'll cope!'

'I'm sure you will, but I have my mobile with me if you need anything.'

I smiled at Josh who was now tipping all my felt pens on to the floor. He was a handful, he was annoying, but he was all right really.

I was just trying to explain to Josh the importance of being quiet when the phone rang again. I rolled my eyes and answered it. It was probably Mum checking up on me. She'd only been gone about ten minutes.

'Hello?'

'Hi, Millie, it's Dad here!'

'Oh, hi!'

'I was wondering if you would like to come to dinner on Thursday night. Don't worry, I've checked and I'm totally free!'

I smiled a smile so huge it took over my entire face. He wanted to go to dinner with *me*! Not with his 'snuggle-bunny', not with a business colleague – with ME! Just me!

'Yes!' I replied, grinning. 'Yes, of course I would!'

'Fantastic! Abby can't wait to see you again.'

Did he just say Abby? What's Abby got to do with our father-daughter dinner?

'Abby?'

'Yes. Oh, didn't I say? Silly me! It's dinner at Abby's. She's going to be cooking specially for us. Isn't that great?'

'Umm . . . yes. Amazing,' I said, feeling my face fall dramatically.

'I'll pick you up at six on Thursday. See you then! Bye!'

'Bye!'

I sighed as I put the phone back on the hook. So much for a father and daughter dinner, and so much for the importance of being quiet – Josh was running down the stairs making aeroplane noises.

* * *

On the way to school next day I told Patrick about the doom ahead. (Sorry, dinner.)

'Really?'

'Yes!'

'Well, you better not attempt the plan again. You'll just give in and pass the salad!'

He sniggered, but I gave him a knowing look which meant, 'You laugh and it'll be the last time you ever do!' He shut up.

'Well, it's lucky I have another plan, then, isn't it?' he said, smiling.

'You do?' I asked. 'What is it?'

'Well, it's so simple, even you could pull it off!'

His eyes twinkled as I lifted my eyebrows. 'Well?'

'All you have to do is keep talking about how amazing your mum is. How great at everything she is, how she's so much better than Abby! You get me?'

'But won't my dad notice?'

'Um . . . I dunno, but it's worth the risk!'

'OK, I guess. New plan to be put into action tomorrow night!

'Good on you, Agent C!'

By the time we reached the school we had the plan completely covered and I was actually feeling quite confident about it. I was feeling so confident in fact, that in history, I decided to tell my super-duper blonde friend, Holly, about it.

'So, what's this great plan you've come up with,

then? Does it involve me?'

I shook my head. 'Don't worry, you don't have to do anything.'

She smiled, looking a little relieved. 'Well, what are you doing?'

'I'm going over to Abby's tomorrow for dinner. I'm going to spend the evening talking about how great my mum is. Hopefully it'll annoy her!'

'Umm . . . is that the target? To annoy her? I thought you wanted to actually get rid of her.'

'I do!'

'Well, talking about your mum isn't going to get her to leave now, is it?'

I thought about that for a moment. It was true, it probably wouldn't achieve anything. Talking about my mum's great cooking, sense of style and kindness wouldn't be enough to get Abby to leave. Maybe it was a start though, maybe it would just get the ball rolling a bit.

'Well, I'm hoping it will just start things off. There'll be other plans after it!'

'Oh, OK then! Hey, you know . . .'

'Girls at the back!' Mrs Newton shouted from the front. 'Quiet please. Get on with the exercise!'

We got back to describing World War Two.

Thursday evening dragged on like a bad Oscars speech. I lay on my bed, listening to some annoyingly catchy song on the radio. I was trying to think of some things to say later, but all that revolved in my head was the chorus of the song currently playing. I sighed. I couldn't think of anything worthwhile to say to Abby about Mum. I was just going to have to hope that once I was there, the words would just pop out of my mouth.

I stared at the clock beside my bed and watched the numbers after the five change, one by one. 5.12 . . . 5.13 . . . 5.14 . . . I sighed. Why was time taking so long to move along?

Josh ran into the room making weird and wacky animal noises, but when he got no reaction out of me he soon left. I heard Rachel screaming a few minutes later. It was something like, 'Just go away will you, you stupid little twit!'

How charming of her, she's always loved Josh. (I'm being sarcastic!)

I must have fallen asleep after that because the next moment I heard Mum calling from downstairs.

'Millie, your father's here!'

'Just a second!' I yelled as I pulled my knee-high boots on. I checked my hair in the mirror and hurried down the stairs (as well as I could in my heels, anyway).

'Aww, Millie!' my dad said, smiling. 'You look gorgeous.'

I blushed and grabbed my coat from the stand in the hall.

'Bye, Mum!' I yelled into the kitchen as I closed the door behind me.

'Have fun!' I heard in reply.

* * *

It didn't take long to get to Abby's. My stomach turned over as we pulled up outside.

Then my dad gave me one of his strange eyebrow-raising looks and said, 'Here we are, then! Let's get inside! I don't know about you, but I'm starving! I could eat a hippopotamus!'

'Well, I'm not in the mood for hippo myself. I hope there's another choice on the menu!'

My dad chuckled. 'Inheriting my sense of humour, Millie? Be afraid. Be very afraid!'

I wrinkled my nose at him. Why was he being so jolly? I didn't like it at all! Don't get me wrong, I don't like it when he's depressed or anything, but I can't stand it either when he has his little moments. The moments when he acts like some of the boys in my class.

My dad opened the car door and practically leapt out of his seat. I sighed and got out slowly, imagining the doom to come.

'Come on, Millie, look lively!' my dad said, grinning as he hurried up to the door. 'Aren't you looking forward to this?'

Oh yes! I was soooo looking forward to sitting at the table watching Dad and Abby eat each other while I got to eat some kind of exotic cat sick. I think *not*! Abby was bound to be just as good at cooking as my little brother. His cakes could break your teeth in a second (he likes to build them out of lego blocks . . . ouch).

I followed my dad up the garden path to the door (i.e., DOOM) and watched as my dad pressed his finger on the bell.

I wasn't really sure whether I was feeling confident or not. I suppose I was, well, a little. I was looking forward to seeing the look on Abby's face and dissecting it bit by bit. The part I wasn't looking forward to seeing was the look on my dad's face as he tried to work out what the hell I was doing and why the hell I was doing it.

Abby beamed at us as she opened the door (though I think it was a beam for Dad rather than me).

'Come on in! Come on in!' she said, smiling. 'Food's almost ready!'

Dad stepped through the doorway, wiping his muddy trainers on the welcome mat. 'I'm starving!' he announced.

Abby showed us through to the dining room, but from the way Dad marched in it was obvious this wasn't his first visit. I scowled to myself. I had to make this evening a success! I had to make Abby doubt things, so that he'd enjoy spending time alone with me again. I just had to get my dad back.

I sat myself down at the table, my eyes wandering around the room, scanning the light blue walls looking for, well, anything really.

My dad took a seat opposite and grinned at me, Cheshire cat style.

'Isn't Abby's artwork amazing?' he asked, waving his

hand at the various framed pieces on the wall. 'Very professional looking, aren't they?'

I lifted my eyes and stared at the pictures on the wall. They were good. No. They were excellent! As much as I hated to admit it, Abby had talent and style.

'They're OK,' I grunted.

I looked round the room. It was all very modern, and very tidy. Everything seemed to have a place and if it wandered out of that place the whole house would fall apart. It couldn't have been more organised. I felt slightly uncomfortable sitting there, in case I made the room untidy.

'Ahh, here we are!' my dad said as Abby entered the room, complete with plates of steaming food. 'Taste buds, prepare to be satisfied!'

I lifted the fork which was lying beside the plate and prepared to dip it into the pasta which Abby had put in front of me. It looked surprisingly good, but I decided it must be a disaster in disguise. It couldn't be nice. It was going to be terrible. I just knew it was.

I scooped up a large mouthful and watched as the steaming blob neared my pursed lips.

'Prepare to meet your doom, Mill!' I said under my breath and shovelled the food into my mouth.

'What do you think, then?' Abby asked me as I swallowed. 'It's an old recipe I dug up.'

It was gorgeous, like a small taste of heaven.

'It's OK,' I grunted, then added quickly, 'but my

mum's is better. She makes it with this vegetable sauce which is just heavenly. It's to die for, really, it is!'

'Oh,' said Abby with a hurt look. 'I'm sure it is.'

My dad gave me a puzzled look as if to say, 'Your mother couldn't cook to save her life. What are you on about?'

Every hungry taste bud in my mouth was telling me to gulp the rest of the plate down as fast as possible, but I just couldn't. I had to stand my ground, so I sat there, twirling the spaghetti strings round my fork and listening to the gentle conversation from across the table.

'So I'm heading up to Barry sometime to present a few pieces of my work . . .' Abby said.

'Hey, Dad!' I interrupted, spotting my chance and taking it. 'Remember when you, Mum and me went to Barry Island together. We had so much fun, didn't we? Mum was so good at the crane machines, she won us all prizes. Remember? That was such a good day!'

'Umm . . . yes,' my dad said, raising his eyebrows. He turned back to face Abby and smiled. 'Are you still planning to have your kitchen done?'

'Yes, next week actually. I'm going over to my sister's this weekend so they can get on with it. It's a bit of a pain really, going there, but they shouldn't take too long.'

'Any idea how long you'll be away, then?' my dad asked as he spooned more pasta into his mouth.

'I'm not quite sure. A few weeks, I suppose. Hopefully less. Whenever it's safe to move back really.'

'Well, you know where I am if you need any help.'

'That's a nice offer, but everything seems to be running smoothly.'

I sighed. How was I supposed to fit my mum into a boring 'falling asleep' conversation like this?

So for the next twenty minutes I sat at the table, finishing my pasta as slowly as humanly possible, listening to the five-star boredom chatter. Blab about work and equally boring things.

I wondered about Kaori, she hadn't said anything else about her dad in school, she'd just been rather quiet. Though, we don't have any lessons alone together, so she hadn't really had an opportunity to tell me anything. I sighed. Poor Kaori.

I spooned the remaining pasta from my plate into my mouth and slowly chewed. Abby and Dad continued to talk and I continued not to listen.

'Oh, I went down the garden centre last week and picked up a selection of bulbs. They're planted out the back. They'll look amazing when they bloom. I think I have the packet somewhere upstairs if you'd like to have a look at that.'

My dad smiled. 'That would be great! You coming, Millie?'

'Umm . . . nah. I'll just wait here.'

'You sure?'

I nodded.

'OK, then!'

So Abby and Dad left the room, whispering to one another. Once they were out of sight I lifted myself from the chair and wandered over to the desk-like thing in the corner. I found my fingers flicking through the various pieces of paper upon it, my eyes scanning the information on them.

Boring, boring, boring!

A series of bills, bank statements and receipts flooded the desk. They were all neatly organised with little tabs separating each one. I sighed. There was nothing.

Then I saw something, sitting in between a receipt for some sort of top and an electricity bill. I smiled a smile so smiley that not even Smiley McSmiley could outsmile me! I was holding a single piece of paper, a photograph, actually. In the picture was Abby, her long hair flowing down her shoulders. She was standing in the garden, purple flowers everywhere. At her feet were three black poodles and one white one. They looked like they were panting dramatically, though that wasn't the interesting part. Next to her, with his arm around her waist, was a tall man with brown hair. He was grinning toothily. On the back, it said: *Poodles with Paul, 13th October.*

If that date was right, then the two-timing sea witch was probably seeing this Paul guy the same time as she was seeing my dad! Just the sort of thing she'd do. She was probably still going out with him.

I scowled at the picture. At that moment I heard the back door open, I hastily put the photograph into my pocket.

Abby and Dad entered the room.

'Coming to watch TV with us, Mill?' Dad said, smiling.

I found myself nodding and following the couple into the living room.

Chapter 6

J is for Jason

The following Saturday I got up early, ready to go shopping with Megan, my quiet yet very fun-to-be-with friend. She was forcing me out on a mega-shopping spree (shock horror) so that she could:

a) get a present for her dad's birthday next week, and

b) go boy hunting. Although Megan is as shy as anything, she is completely boy mad! Well, as long as they're at a distance.

'Hey, Mill!' Megan sniggered, pulling me towards her by my brand new charm bracelet. 'Look at that boy over there!'

I followed her gaze across the shopping centre to a group of four boys that were hanging around outside some cookie shop. They were all holding identical black and white skateboards that had skulls across the bottom and they were all wearing the same sort of baggy green combats and black hoodies. The techno lighting lit up all of their faces as they stood there, trying to look cool.

'Which one?'

'Him, with the skateboard!'

I lifted my eyebrows a metre off my head and sighed.

She carried on staring and giggled to me. 'I think he's cute!'

'Go speak to him, then!'

She pouted her lips, spread out her fingers, shivered and firmly shook her head until she proved too dizzy to carry on.

'As if! He'd probably call me mucus or a loser or something like that and then I'd feel so bad that I'd burst into a flood of tears and spend the rest of my days hiding in the nearest toilet. Nope, it's probably better if I just stare at him now and hope he comes over to see me. Then, if he doesn't I'll just go home and gaze into space for hours on end!'

I rolled my eyes and marvelled at how shy my friend could be.

'Oh for pity's sake, Megs, just go over there. I mean, if he hates you, then you'll never see him again anyway so it doesn't really matter, does it?'

'Well, if you're the queen of love, then how come you didn't talk to that boy you liked, the one you saw the other week? You obviously liked him, you talked about him enough.'

That left me tongue-tied.

'Ha! See! It's not that easy when you're in the situation, is it, Mill? Come on, let's just go!'

Megan picked up her bag of various accessories

and started to head towards the double doors.

'No!' I insisted, stamping an impatient foot on the marbled floor. I mean, I wasn't going to let her wander out the door and leave a possible soulmate behind in the dust. 'Which one do you like? We're going to talk to him!'

'No!' Megan called after me, bringing her one hundred and one newly purchased items along with her. 'Stop! We're not, please!'

She couldn't stop me though because I was as determined as ever. Megan may be a shy old fool, but I'm certainly not! I could hear her clip-clopping along behind me, *way* behind me.

'Hi!' I yelled in their direction. All four stunned blond boys spun round to see a crazy curly-haired girl (i.e., me) marching towards them followed by a shady figure who was holding a Tammy bag in front of her face.

'I'm Millie and this is my mate Megan!'

The boys looked past me and stared puzzled at the partly obscured girl who appeared to be slowly edging backwards.

'Megs!' I called.

She peered round the fashionable mask and smiled weakly at the gang of gobsmacked lads. The tall one in front was cute and he smiled at me . . . and that's when I realised – it was him! Blond hair sparkling under the glow of the light, perfect white teeth lined up in a toothpaste-advert smile. The curve of his lips ending in one hundred percent gorgeous dimples. I melted. It was him! No, not any old him! The him that had stepped off the bus the other week, the him that had winked at me, the him I had fantasised about afterwards! The him I'd talked to all my friends about so much, the him I'd talked to Patrick about.

Patrick . . . what about Patrick?

Dream Boy winked at me, as if to say he remembered and then said, 'I'm Matt, this is Mike, Will and Jason.'

Megan tugged on my jumper and mumbled slowly and quietly, 'That's him, the Jason one!'

I sighed at her, Megan was pushed to the side of my mind as I thought about how it must be fate for me to meet up with Dream Boy again and now I had a name to match that gorgeous face. Matt.

'He's sexy, isn't he?' Megan said, grinning.

Personally I thought that Jason was just about as attractive as Michael Jackson on a bad surgery day (maybe even worse). Hey, it was her choice if out of a gang of mostly gorgeous guys she had singled out the weedy wart. Hmm . . . I mean, how could she prefer Jason over Matt?

'Like your skirt!' Matt winked, looking down.

I had almost completely forgotten about my minier-than-mini-skirt (one to put Kylie Minogue to shame). To tell you the truth, it barely covered my knickers. Quite breezy, but while we were in the shopping centre, it wasn't really any different from a pair of jeans.

I blushed and desperately tried to pull it down slightly. He reached out and grabbed my arm gently, and said, 'Leave it, I like it like that!'

This lead to more blushing and even more tummy turning.

So Megs and I spent another three hours shopping with Matt and his gang. I'm not positive whether Megan actually plucked up the courage to say more than a few garbled words to Jason, but he was all she could talk about for ages afterwards.

'*And* he's a great skateboarder. He showed me some of his moves, *and* he plays the guitar, *and* he plays the piano *and* the drums!'

I smiled at her and listened. My mind was ticking over with the image of Matt, the sound of his voice. He was my soulmate, I was sure. But if he was my soulmate, what was Patrick? Was he just a friend after all?

I was so confused, it seemed so simple. I fancied Matt so I should go out with him. Obviously my feelings for Patrick were as a friend. I'd just got a bit confused.

But if that's all it was, why had things started to feel so strange with him?

I couldn't get lovebird Megs to stop grinning from ear to ear either and it was the most talkative my shy and secretive friend has ever been in her entire life. Phew! I couldn't get a word in edgeways which is hard to get used to. I mean, although Megan's not shy around me, she's never *that* loud.

So now Kaori and Megan both had proper boyfriends. I mean, Matt and I had exchanged numbers (he wrote his on the back of his chewing gum wrapper – how romantic), but I wasn't raising my hopes. After all, a gorgeous boy like that would have girls queuing for miles for just five minutes with him. Plus the Patrick problem was still under careful consideration. I didn't know whether I was even going to call Matt, but he was so gorgeous!

Did he really like me? It was more than likely I'd get my heart broken (or shattered). I suppose meeting him properly had made me more realistic.

I was lying on my bed, stretching my arms into the air and staring into space. It was the perfect way to relax after an interesting (and exhausting) five-hour shopping spree. Somewhere at the back of my mind, I had the smallest inkling that my feet were going to ache for quite some time (like until the sky fell down). I couldn't believe I'd met and spoken to Dream Boy (now known as Matt). And he liked my skirt! *Blush blush!*

I was pretty much alone in the house. Rachel was round at her boyfriend's house (that's where she always was these days, what could they possibly do that takes every minute of every day?). DM was at the garden centre, where I assume he was buying things for the garden, though I could be wrong. Josh was at his friend's house for the day, so, all in all, the house was very quiet, just me and Mum.

There was a loud knock at the door and I heard Mum call.

'Millie! Are you ready to go to your father's?'

I sighed to myself. It was four o'clock and I was totally worn out. Of course I didn't want to go to my dad's. He obviously didn't want me there, after all he had told me not to come at the usual time of half-past twelve because he was going shopping with Abby.

Anyway, I was sick of stupid Dad, I was sick of his stupid irritating young girlfriend and I was sick of that stupid house with the stupid mess and the stupid constant cold. I would have been more than happy if I never set foot there ever again (apart from not seeing Mr Goggle. I'd miss him, even if he chews up my homework, pees in my room, barks at all hours of the flipping night and scoffs himself silly with all my delicious food . . . never mind). And obviously Abby would be there.

I sat up straight, as an interesting thought popped into my head. Hadn't Abby said last Thursday that she was having her kitchen redone this week? Hadn't she said she would be staying at her sister's for a while? Did that mean she was leaving? Did that mean she wouldn't be there? Did it? Did it? Would I get some time alone with Dad? Just me and him?

I felt myself break into a wide grin and bounced off the bed.

'Ready, Mum!' I yelled, hoping and praying that I was right and Abby would be about as visible as the Invisible Man when I got over there.

'I'll see you on Monday, then, Mill!' Mum yelled from the car which suddenly seemed so far away. I just stood in the driveway, hoping that Abby wouldn't be there once I got inside.

'Millie!'

I heard my dad's call from the house behind me. I waited a moment, listening for a female voice to follow, but there was none.

'Come inside, silly!' he called. 'You'll freeze if you stay out here!'

It was rather chilly outside, but I wouldn't have said it was freezing. That was just Dad, overreacting as per usual. So, I turned myself round and headed inside to the almost freezing house. Apparently Dad hadn't got round to installing the new boiler yet and I was beginning to wish he'd decided to do that before he'd taken out the old one.

'No Abby?' I said matter-of-factly.

'No, she's gone to her sister's while her kitchen's being redone. She won't be back for two weeks or so.'

I felt my chilly lips form a silly smile and then wondered what would be the normal way to react. Should I pretend to be sorry? Should I say nothing?

I just decided to ignore the fact and try to enjoy the time with my dad.

'So, are we going to do anything this weekend?' I said, beaming at him.

'Aww. Sorry, pumpkin, but I'm overwhelmed with work. I thought that since Abby was away this weekend it would be a good idea to catch up on some unfinished paperwork.'

I groaned. Then paused. Then groaned louder.

'What's wrong, Millie? Have you got something stuck in your throat?'

I rolled my eyes and groaned again, a groan to put our vacuum cleaner to shame.

'You wouldn't want to hang out with an old fogey like me anyway. Why don't you call one of your friends? Hola, or Kaoria or Patty or someone?'

'That's Holly, Kaori and Patrick actually!'

'That's what I said, Mill.'

So I wandered upstairs, leaving my dad alone with his precious paperwork.

After umm . . . three minutes in the quietest house imaginable, I decided I couldn't take the boredom any more. I needed to talk to someone sane (i.e., anyone that wasn't a member of my loonier than loony family). My attention span (umm . . . what was I saying?!) seemed to be at it's lowest this particular October morning. Maybe because my subconscious was ticking and tocking away, trying (and absolutely failing) to think up another brain-teasing idea for Abby's eviction. How could I prove she was two-timing Dad? The photo wasn't enough.

Anyway, I couldn't concentrate and this led me to the conclusion that if I went about calling one of my louder mates (i.e., Lucinda or Holly), our conversation would end up with some sort of bust-up because I wasn't listening to a goddam thing. I wasn't really tempted to call Megan either. I mean, if I heard the name Jason more than umm . . . once, then I think I'd have to personally remove him from existence.

After mulling over my limited options I decided to call Kaori. She'd been so quiet in school the past few days. It was my duty, as a good friend, to put her before myself and try and help her out. It would also be a good way to get my mind off my dad and his obsessive Millie-neglect disorder.

So I picked up the phone on the landing and dialled Kaori's number.

We arranged to meet at the café down the road, because it looked like it would be getting dark soon. I certainly didn't want her to come over to mine. I try and avoid having friends over at my dad's as much as possible because it's so messy. I get very embarrassed. (And of course, I won't clean it up myself – I'm a teenager: cleaning is not in my job description.) And it wouldn't have been a very good idea to go to Kaori's with her dad being there and everything.

So I yelled a short 'bye' in the direction of my dad's study, waited while he completely ignored me, then I headed out the door.

I wandered down the road, staring at the blue and grey swirling sky. I had to pull my black coat around myself as tightly as was humanly possible (or is that coatly possible?). I was stupid enough to leave my jumper inside.

It was almost five o'clock as I walked towards the café, glancing across the park (if you could call it that – it was more a square of grass with three swings on) on my way. It looked busier than usual (meaning I wasn't the only neglected teen out and about). There was a girl, hunched on a mouldy bench, swaying back and forth.

Oh no! This isn't good, I thought, as the girl lifted the hood of her jacket to reveal Kaori drenched in tears so thick that it was hard to make out her face at all.

I ran over to her, feeling my feet slowly sink into muddy grass beneath them.

'Kaori! Are you OK?' I panted (it's a long sprint from the road to the mangled benches).

Her reply was another endless series of depressing sobs.

'Come on, Kazza, are you OK?'

She wiped her dripping nose on her purple sleeve and looked up at me.

'Of . . . course . . . I'm not . . . OK, Mill! What . . . kind of question . . . is . . . is that?!' she stuttered between sniffs. 'My dad's having a . . . a . . . an affair!'

I sat myself on the bench beside her and slipped my arm round her shoulders. She leant over to me and buried her head in my coat.

'It's OK, Kaz! It'll all turn out fine!'

She shook her head feebly and burst into another fit of hiccupy tears.

'I don't see how it can!' she said, sniffing.

'These sorts of things happen all the time.' I sighed. 'It's awful, but it usually turns out OK.'

'Only usually?' she asked.

'Does your mum know about it?'

She quickly shook her head and fixed her big brown eyes on my small green ones.

'She can't find out! They'd get divorced!'

'What are you going to do, then?'

She fell silent (apart from the odd sniffle every now and then).

'I don't know,' she said finally.

I sighed. I would have offered to help her myself, but I would never have been able to come up with a plan for her as well as for me.

'You'll think of something, Kaz,' I said, smiling. 'You always do.'

In less than a second I had a pair of warm Kaori arms around my neck. 'Thanks for listening,' she said, drying her tears on my shoulder. 'Don't tell anyone, though! Nobody.'

I nodded, what else could I do? What more could I say? I just hugged her close and prayed for a miracle for her.

'How's your plan going, then?' she asked me, tears fading.

'Plan?' I said, raising my eyebrows.

'Yeah, you know, the one to get rid of your dad's girlfriend?'

I gasped. 'How do you know about that?'

'Holly told us.'

I rolled my eyes. Was Holly completely incapable of keeping a secret?

'Oh, well . . . it isn't going too well. Not much success yet.'

She nodded.

I pulled Kaori closer and hugged her.

'We're a right old pair, aren't we, Kaz?'

She lifted her head and smiled at me.

'Yep! We are indeed, Mill!'

As I wandered back to the house I felt my coat pocket vibrating. I picked up the trembling mobile and groaned as I saw the word 'Megan' flashing on the screen.

'Hi, Megs,' I said, very unenthusiastically.

'Hi, Mill! Guess where Jason's taking me next week?'

'I give up.'

'The cinema! Isn't that soooo romantic!'

I smiled. 'Yeah Meg, that's great.'

'Yeah, well, I've got to go, I need to call him to confirm.'

And the phone went dead.

* * *

Back at the house, Dad was sitting in precisely the same spot I'd left him, except there was a mountain of papers on the floor and half a pizza on the desk.

So after getting myself a glass of Coke and a few slices of warmed-up pizza, I slipped upstairs to practise my kissing technique. Yes, I know it may be sad, but hey, it could help transform me from a weedy swot to a desirable sex goddess and my stuffed duck is kind of cool to practise on, in a yellow-ducky kind of way.

I just couldn't believe my luck at the moment (bad luck, that is). I could only assume that my fairy godmother had somehow misplaced her glitzy magic wand (or her glitzy magic brain). Trust me to get stuck with the ditzy one!

After lying on my rather lumpy old mattress for twenty minutes, thinking about the past, present and future of my stink of a life in the pitch dark, I settled down to go to sleep and let another eight or nine pointless hours pass by. Why couldn't my dad just get rid of Abby? Why couldn't I just ask Patrick how he felt? Why couldn't Kaori at least attempt to talk to her dad about the whole thing?

I suppose it's hard for her. I remember how awful I felt when my parents got divorced. It was only four years ago and I thought my whole world was going to end. If only I didn't have so much to deal with myself, then I'd be able to help her properly, give her the support she needs.

If only, huh! I was beginning to get the picture that someone, somewhere, didn't like me.

In the morning I was woken by my dashing prince – I wish! It was Mr Goggle, slobbering me from head to foot.

'Geroff!' I yelled between unwanted snogs. 'Geroff!' I pushed the furry mutt off my stomach and sighed.

'Good morning to you too!' I said.

I wandered downstairs to eat Cheerios. It was then I heard the conversation – the conversation that sparked a very good idea.

My dad was on the phone in the other room.

'Now, now, calm down, Abby! It's not the end of the world . . . Yes, I know . . . I'm sure . . . yes . . . yes. Well, surely you can go and pick them up . . . Ah, I see. OK, well, I'm a bit busy with all this paperwork, I have to finish it by Tuesday . . . Yes, I know you need them. There's no way you can get away? Well, I suppose I'll pick them up for you . . . What about the key? . . . I could leave it outside? OK, then. You'd better . . . OK, I love you too. Bye.'

I shovelled another mouthful of Cheerios into my mouth and listened as my dad came fumbling round the corner.

'I have to go and sort something out for Abby. She's trapped at her sister's and the taps she's ordered haven't arrived. I'm going to have to collect them for her so the builders can fit them. You want to drive up with me?'

'Why's it so important for her kitchen to be redone? What's wrong with the old one?' I asked. 'Is it in a really bad state so it has to be done quickly?'

'Well, not really, it's just . . . well, it's a bit out of date and . . .'

Dad sat himself down at the table opposite me and sighed.

'You see, she's selling her house and the estate agent suggested a new kitchen would make it sell a lot faster,' he said.

I felt my heart leap inside me. It wouldn't stop somersaulting. Abby wasn't going to move in with us, was she? How long had Dad been seeing her? Was it really that serious? I don't know if I'd be able to survive with another woman living in the house. It would be too weird, too scary. Dad wouldn't do that to me, would he?

No, he couldn't, even if he wanted to, this house couldn't take an extra person really. It was too small.

'I'm planning on selling this house too . . .'

No, he wouldn't, he couldn't sell the house. It was right next to Patrick, and close to the school. Where would he move to and what would be the point of moving, anyway?

When the realisation came it brought the feeling of sickness with it.

Abby selling her house, Dad selling his . . .

Dad cleared his throat and went on, '. . . and Abby and I are going to buy a bigger house somewhere. We can afford it if we combine our money.'

Was there a lump in my throat or was it just the Cheerios on their way down?

'I'm sorry I didn't tell you sooner, I was just waiting for the right time. So, are you coming?'

I couldn't let Abby take my dad further away from me! What if I couldn't see him as much? How far away was he going to move? There weren't many bigger houses round here.

I swallowed my cereal and sighed. At least if I went with Dad now, there would be no one but me and him.

'Sure, I haven't got anything better to do.'

He smiled. 'Well, be ready in five!'

It wasn't long before we were settled in Dad's car, driving down the motorway, listening to some old rubbish of my dad's on CD. I cringed as he sang along to the words.

Millie! This is what you wanted, I told myself. A little time alone with your dad, and now you have it, you don't appreciate it at all.

But his singing was awful!

'Now it should be round here somewhere,' my dad said, turning down the volume. 'Get the map out of the glove compartment, would you, Mill?'

I reached forward and pulled out the small *A–Z*. I handed it to my dad.

'I'm not a magician, Millie! I can't drive and read

the map at the same time! You'll have to look it up for me. Now, look at the back for . . . now what was the street again?'

I rolled my eyes. Memory like a sieve!

We did eventually find the street where the manager of Ben's Builders lived. If they had tried to make it impossible to find them they'd almost succeeded.

Dad looked at the beefy guy who opened the door and smiled.

'Hello,' he said. 'I'm Mr Addicott. I'm here to collect a key for Abby Turner, 42 Gregory Avenue?'

The man grunted once and disappeared. When he returned, he was holding a small silver key. He handed it to Dad and stood in the doorway, his large arms folded across his chest.

'So,' my dad said, sighing. 'You'll be coming over to the house tomorrow around three?'

The man nodded slowly.

'Great, well, I'll leave the key in the soil in the right window box. The taps will be inside.'

The man nodded again.

'Well, thank you!' my dad said, rubbing his fingers over the key. 'Thank you very much.'

On the way back to the car, Dad sighed. 'Charming bloke,' he said.

I smiled. 'Being sarcastic, are we, Dad?'

He grinned back at me. 'Of course not, Millie, you know I don't approve of sarcasm.'

I looked at Dad and that's when it clicked. Abby's house, no one there, key outside . . . It was all too perfect.

It was almost midday when we found ourselves back in the car on the way to collect the taps, Dad's singing circling round, killing everything. Oh well, I may not be the biggest fan of his Elvis impression, but it was better than watching him with Abby. Like a million times better. It was just me and Dad.

Dad had a bit of a go at the man behind the desk at Kitchen World.

'And why didn't you deliver them as you promised?'

'I'm very sorry, sir!'

'I know you're sorry, I want to know why they weren't delivered!'

'It won't happen again!'

'I'm sure it won't, but why did it happen this time?'

In the end the poor sweating employee explained that their main driver had been sick and so lots of deliveries had been disturbed. My dad just grunted as though it wasn't a good enough excuse. Then, he lifted the box of taps from the counter and headed towards the door.

'Come on, Mill! Let's get these to Abby's!'

The next part of the journey was just as tedious as the last, though I took my time watching where we were going as my dad drove. I would need to remember the exact location of Abby's house if my plan was to work. After all, how could it succeed if I couldn't find the house?

'Here we are, Mill. Abby's humble abode!' Dad said as he pulled up outside the house.

I smiled at him smugly as I climbed out of the car.

He opened the boot and lifted out the heavy box of taps, crumpling his back as he did it.

'Millie, could you carry these for me please? My back's not what it used to be!'

I rolled my eyes, but he didn't appear to notice. Probably because he was too busy moaning about the back problems he doesn't have. He always uses that excuse to make me carry things. The cheek.

So I carried the taps up the garden path to the front door, Dad strolling along in front, whistling and twirling the key round his finger.

It didn't take long for him to unlock the door, grab the taps off me and shove them inside. It took him all of half a second, then he turned, smiled at me and said, 'Well, Millie, let's get going!'

'Umm . . . Dad. Shouldn't you, like, lock the door?'

'I was just about to do that!' he said, covering. 'Give me a second, Mill!'

I rolled my eyes again and watched as he fiddled with the key. Once the door was fully locked I watched Dad place the key in the window box, just buried under the soil on the surface.

I felt a smile form on my face. Tomorrow was going to be a good day.

Chapter 7

K is for Knotting stomachs and L is for Love or lust?

Once back in the comfort (not) of my dad's house I ran up to my room to call Patrick. After all, I wasn't going to set up the plan all by myself. I was going to need help.

'I have to get rid of her now more than ever,' I said.

'Why?'

'Because my dad told me they're selling both their houses and are going to move into a bigger house together.'

'Whoa! Really? Where?'

'That's the problem, I don't know where. Could be in Australia or something.'

'Unlikely.'

'But possible! There are no big houses near here, and it's bad enough now – I know I'll end up not seeing him as often, and when I do, she'll be there. I'll never get to spend time alone with him. I have a plan though.'

'What happened to *my* plan?' he whined.

'What plan?'

'The talk-about-your-mother plan?'

'You can hardly call that a plan. I mean, it was hardly going to achieve anything, was it? Be realistic, Patrick!'

'Fine! What's this plan, then?'

'Well, it's not actually a fully formulated plan,' I admitted.

I heard Patrick sniggering on the other end of the phone.

'Shut up! It's way better than yours anyway!'

'Well? What *have* you got, then?'

'We're going to her house tomorrow lunch-time. I don't know what we're going to do yet though.'

'So we stand outside her house and hope that by some miracle the door opens and an idea jumps out at us yelling, "Here I am, I'm an idea! Take me! Take me!"?'

'OK, OK. Easy on the sarcasm there, Pat! Don't get so ahead of yourself. No, we're not just going to stand around outside. I'm not *completely* stupid, you know!'

I heard him mumble, 'Whatever.'

'Oi! Cheeky! Well, I know where there's a spare key! You see, last week, while I was having dinner at Abby's, I found this photo!'

'Photo? What photo?'

'Shut up and let me finish, Mr Impatient! Well, it was a photo of Abby with another man. So, what I thought was that we could go over and have a look for more evidence of her two-timing!'

'What do you need more evidence for? If it's a picture of her with another man, then it proves she's cheating on him!'

'Umm . . . hello??? Anyone alive in there? It could be *anyone*! I'm not going to muck it up.'

'OK! OK! Fair enough, take a chill pill, Mill!'

'Ha ha, very witty, Pat! See you tomorrow!'

'Bye!'

I smiled as I put the phone down. Patrick was a friend, the very best friend I could ever ask for. He wasn't going to be more than that, he wasn't going to be my boyfriend. I was going to put that whole ridiculous idea to sleep. It had been stupid, but now I was back on Earth.

The rest of my day was spent watching some obscure science programme on the television with Mr Goggle flopped out across my lap. Dad was just sat in the study all day, slowly signing and filing page by page.

The afternoon drifted by. My phone lay silent. Nobody called, there were no text messages and it was altogether very, well, dull! I sighed to myself. I had a load of maths homework to do, so I slung Mr Goggle on the floor, bless him, and got to work on algebraic equations. There I stayed for an hour, quietly finishing formulas and equations. I don't mind algebra actually, it's quite fun when you get into it.

Later that evening, though, I was surprised by an unexpected phone call.

I was lying on the sofa in a strange manner, feet

curled up, arms loose, watching an American sitcom. I sighed as my mobile in the corner of the room started playing its annoying tune. I quickly pushed Mr Goggle aside and ran over to the phone.

'Hello.'

'Hi, Millie, it's Matt!'

Ohmygod, Matt!

'Umm . . . hi!' I said, practically speechless. He was calling *me*?

'I just thought that maybe you lost my phone number so I called instead.'

'Yeah, I did lose it!' I lied through my teeth, hoping that he'd believe me. I pictured him at his house on the phone. He was totally knee-knockingly GORGEOUS!

I shook the image of Patrick's face out of my head as soon as it appeared there.

'I was thinking we could go to this disco on Saturday. It's at eight, I'll pick you up, want to come?'

Humm . . . yes or no? Yes or no?

'Can I bring some mates?'

'Um . . . I guess!'

Yes or no? Yes or no?

'Well, Millie?'

It's make your mind up time, Millie! Come on, yes or no?

'Yeah, sounds like fun.'

'Cool, see you then!'

I switched my phone off and smiled. Did I make the right choice?

Of course I did! You'd have to be a complete idiot to turn down a boy like Matt, or be a hundred per cent blind! But a second opinion might help . . .

'Hiya, Hollz!'

'Hey, Mill!'

'Umm . . . I'm kind of in a sticky situation.'

'Oh yes?'

'Yes.'

'Well?'

'Umm . . . it's, like, a boy thing.'

'What's a boy again, Mill?' she said sarcastically.

'Ha ha, Hollz. I'm serious!'

'Well, is it the thing about . . .'

'No, you can't possibly know.'

'Oh. What, then?'

'Well, it's kind of exciting. You remember the boy I saw on the way home from school a while back?'

'Yeah, Matt.'

'Yeah, well . . . hey, how did you know he was called Matt?'

'Megan told me.'

'Oh.'

Well, that had ruined my big 'shock, shock, you really won't believe this' moment.

'You met him in town?'

'Well, yes. But more than that!'

'What?'

'He's asked me to a disco on Saturday.'

'Whoa! Really?'

'Yeah, but well, do you think I should go?'

'Umm . . . of course!!! Why not? He's totally gorgeous, well, according to you.'

'Yes, yes he is, isn't he! Fine, I will go and I will have a smashing time.'

'You do that!'

'Yeah, there's something else.'

'Oh yes?'

I hesitated. Why was I having this urge to tell her all about Patrick? What a mistake that would be.

'You still there, Mill?'

I shook myself out of my daydream. 'Yeah, yeah I am.'

'Well?'

'Oh, it doesn't matter. See you'

I sighed as I put the phone down. What was the point of telling her? There was nothing to tell. It was all over with Patrick, it was out of my mind. We were just going to be friends. He wasn't boyfriend material. I would have an amazing time at the disco with gorgeous Matt. It would be an evening to let my hair down and forget all about my silly old Dad and his horrible girlfriend.

I decided I'd call Patrick and tell him all about my glamorous date with Dream Boy, to share my excitement with him. So I picked the phone back up and dialled his number.

This is the second time I've called him today, I thought to myself smiling.

'Hiya, Pat!'

'Hey Mill, you watching the game?'

'Umm . . . no. I have better things to do with my life.'

'Well, I am! It's a really good match!'

Well, that was Patrick's subtle 'I'm in the middle of a football game so go away' comment. I rolled my eyes very unsympathetically. I didn't care, he was going to listen to my news, football game or not!

'Well, I just called to tell you something.'

'No, no, tackle him! Yes . . . yes . . . shoot . . . go on, you can make that shot! Go on!'

'Umm . . . Pat? I called to tell you something!'

'What did you say?'

'I called to tell you something!'

'Ooooh,' he said, excited. 'Is it interesting?'

'Well, I think it is.'

'Don't tell me, you're finally marrying that old Mr Gardener from down the road?'

I laughed. 'Yeah, that's the one, you know me too well.'

'That I do, and I like every bit.'

I felt my stomach flip over, somersaulting one time too many.

'Well, what did you really want to say?'

'Umm . . . well . . .'

And then it hit me, like a wet flannel in the morning. I didn't want Patrick to know about me and Matt. Why? I wasn't really sure. I was just suddenly aware that I didn't want Patrick to know.

'Yes?' he said.

'Umm . . . nothing. I'll . . . I'll talk to you tomorrow!'

So I slammed the phone down and stared at myself in the mirror.

'What is wrong with you?' I asked the figure staring back. But all it did was mimic me.

I went to bed that night wondering about Patrick and Matt. If I didn't want Patrick to know about Matt, then that must mean that I did really like him as more than a friend. And hiding from those feelings just wasn't going to help. Pretending wasn't going to get me anywhere. It was doing my head in. I was going to have to accept it and talk to him. And that scared me like crazy.

Chapter 8

M is for Missions and *N* is for Nit-picking Patrick

The next morning a familiar face greeted me. A familiar face full of doggy drool.

'Good morning to you!' I said as I lifted him off the bed and placed him on the floor.

Actually, this morning was the complete opposite of good, downright bogus in fact. I mean, I was tired, hungry and cold (normal symptoms of Monday morning). But what was much, much worse was, as I made my way down the stairs, I suddenly realised I'd forgotten to revise for the very important French test later.

How can one be expected to revise when one has so many troubling dilemmas to face? Teachers just don't seem to realise that it's nearly impossible to complete all the work they set us. I picked up the book, as I ate my Cheerios and stared blankly at the various verbs and then closed it again. Simple as pie . . . umm . . . not!

I reluctantly packed my muddy school bag and swung my coat on. Then I headed out the door in a doubly bad mood. Monday mornings, huh! Who needs them?

'Hi, Millie!' I heard Patrick call from behind.

I continued to walk, not even bothering to turn back.

'Slow down!' Patrick yelled. 'What's up with you?'

'Monday . . . dog . . . French test!' I muttered.

'Bad day?

I nodded. I mean, boy, was *that* an understatement.

'We still going over to Abby's at lunch?' He was smiling a bit too perkily.

I nodded. 'Bit keen, aren't you?'

'No, just looking forward to spending lunch with you.'

That made me smile.

'Would you want to go out for chips after school?'

I thought for a moment. What was up with Patrick anyway? Was he having the same weird thoughts? We never went out for chips. The last time that happened must have been when we were teeny-weeny and Patrick shut his hand in the car door. Mum said the only thing to cure it was fish and chips, which was a bit ironic really because Patrick had only blown his hand up to the size of a watermelon because he left his furry toy fish in the back of our old Ford Estate.

He smiled at me again. 'Then maybe we can go and see a film after!'

I turned to look at him.

Don't ignore your feelings, Millie, I told myself. Let him in. Let him see.

'Umm . . . well . . .' I began.

'Please?' he said with his heart-melting smile. 'I'd

really like to go with you.'

'I'll think about it,' I said with a cheeky side grin.

This was good enough for Patrick and we continued to march to school. I still had the French test looming ahead.

'Camilla!' Marisol called from behind.

Great! The most popular girl in the year, with the bright blond hair, perfect figure and big blue eyes. She insists on calling me Camilla, even though I can't stand the name. She calls me a swot even though the definition of *swot* is 'one who studies extensively'. I mean, had I even attempted to revise for the French test? No! I may get more As than Bs, but that doesn't make me a swot.

I didn't say anything. I just stared at the ground and scuffed my shoes on the grass.

'Oi! Swot face! You're looking extra disgusting today.'

'At least she doesn't reek of cigarette smoke all the time and she's not going to flunk out of school and become some stinky loser that works in the chippy!' Patrick yelled at her, springing to my defence.

I watched as Marisol brushed a stray hair from her face and walked off.

'You shouldn't put up with her you know, Mill! She's just jealous of you!'

I looked up at Patrick and smiled. No one had ever stood up for me before, no one usually cared. But Patrick had shown her, and it left me with a warm feeling inside, knowing that he cared. And at that moment, something inside me just wanted to smother him in kisses.

I realised I didn't want Matt, it was Patrick I wanted. If only I could bring myself to tell him.

The rest of the morning passed by as usual, I failed the French test with flying colours. It was only after I had given my paper in that I remembered the French for skirt was *jupe* and not *Rock*, which is actually German.

When the bell rang for lunch I gathered my things together and Patrick and I headed up to the gates.

'You sure you want to do this, then?' he said, turning to look at me.

I nodded. 'You bet! This is too perfect a chance to miss, Pat!'

He turned away. Actually, I don't think he was feeling particularly happy about the idea of breaking into a house. Though, it wasn't really breaking in if we had the key, now was it?

We didn't say much on the way, every time Patrick started to say something, I had to shut him up so I could remember where to go. After all, I had never walked there before.

'I think it's this way,' I said, turning down a narrow alley.

Patrick stopped at the entrance and screwed up his face.

'Are you sure? It doesn't look very friendly, and it doesn't look like it goes anywhere.'

'Well, looks can be deceiving, Patrick! This is the way.'

'I don't believe you!'

I rolled my eyes madly. 'Why, Patrick?' I said. 'Why on earth would I be taking you down a narrow alley without a reason? Why?'

He shrugged. 'I don't know. I'm just an innocent victim of your evil plot!'

I smiled, 'Yes, Patrick, I'm taking you down here to cover you in slime and gut you like a fish! Please beware. Now, you coming?'

He shrugged. 'I guess.'

So we headed down the alley and it wasn't long before we were standing outside the familiar shape of Abby's humble abode.

'This is it!' I said, grinning madly, an ear to ear sort of grin. 'Got something to say to me, Patrick?'

'You're right and I'm an idiot.'

'Thank you, Pat, for confirming what we've both known our whole lives. Now, let's do some work!'

We bounced up the drive to the front door and I grinned at him as I removed the key from its hiding place in the window box.

'OK, Mill,' he sighed as the door swung open. 'What are we looking for?'

'Anything that suggests she's having an affair. I don't care what, anything.'

'Another photo?'

'Maybe, just get looking. We won't have long,

I mean, we do have to walk back.'

'What if the builders come?'

'They're not meant to be coming until three. We have plenty of time.'

'What if someone sees us?'

'Who would see us?' I sighed.

'I don't know, an old lady peering out of her window.'

'We have a key, Patrick.'

So we stumbled inside. Patrick went upstairs and I decided to take another look in the dining room desk. Maybe there would be more photos, or a letter or something.

After ten minutes of searching I hadn't found much. Patrick hadn't emerged so I guess he hadn't found anything either. Then, what can only be described as fate, stepped in.

The phone rang. I froze.

'Millie! Do we answer that?' Patrick yelled from upstairs.

'No – of course not! We're not meant to be here. Just ignore it and keep searching!'

'OK!'

After about the seventh ring, a recorded message of Abby's sprung into life.

'Hi, I'm not here to take your call at the moment. Please leave a message after the tone and I'll get right back to you. Bye!'

'Hiya babes.'

I stopped in my tracks and tuned into the call.

'Don't worry, I'm not completely stupid. I do know you're not there. I just thought I'd leave you a nice message for when you come back. How's your kitchen looking? I'll have to pop over and see it sometime. OK, well. Love you, babes. Bye!'

A smile spread across my face. 'Patrick, we have lift off!'

It didn't take us long to put everything back where we had found it. In five minutes it looked as though no one had ever been there. I shut the door, locked it, but just as I was about to put the key in the window box again, I had an idea.

'Millie, what are you doing?' Patrick asked, frowning as I slipped the silver key into my coat pocket.

'The builders are coming over later. Wouldn't it just be awful if they couldn't get in the house?' I said, with a wicked smile.

'Millie, you are too evil for words.'

'I know.' I grinned. 'I know!'

Chapter 9

O is for Only a disco and P is for Patrick's reaction

We headed back to school, my face grinning like the cat that got the cream. I was feeling fantastically happy after setting up the plan. If it could keep Abby away for longer, then I would be ecstatic.

But how would Dad feel about it? Oh, he could survive a bit longer without Abby, couldn't he? And the news of the affair? Yes, that would hurt him, but you have to be cruel to be kind sometimes. He had to know.

'Hey, Pat, we're going back over to Abby's after school tonight. I want to check if the builders have gone.'

'Do we have to? I mean, I kind of have this thing I'm meant to be doing at this place with this person,' Patrick lied, scratching the back of his head with his grubby hand. He smiled at me in the goofiest way possible, giving me a full frontal display of his entire showcase of teeth. It disappeared straight away once he saw the stern and definite 'no no' look on my face.

'Patrick! I was not born yesterday and I confirm again what I said last week. You are positively the *worst* liar in the known universe! If you were busy, then why did you ask me to go with you for chips and the cinema?'

He sulked dramatically and scuffed his shoes along the pavement.

'Well, *thee who wasn't born yesterday*, seeing as you didn't seem too enthusiastic about coming out I made other plans. I now have something really important to do.'

'What's that, then? Bathing your orang-utan?'

He threw in a fake laugh and after scratching his bottom twice, stuck the diseased hand on my left shoulder. 'It's very exclusive!'

'Yeah!' I muttered sarcastically. 'Exclusive, being you and your TV!'

'I don't *have* to come, you know! I'm sick of helping you out with all your family problems. I need a day off from being your friend. It's a twenty-four-hour job these days.'

My heart stopped for a moment as I thought his words over. For some reason, it cut me deep. Was that what he really thought?

'Is not!' I said in my defence.

'Is too!'

'Fine. Don't come. I'm not in the mood for getting in *another* argument.'

I was silent the rest of the way. Patrick pretended to

look at his dirt-infested nails and I just stared at the floor. Thank you, Patrick, for raining on my parade!

Eventually, he broke the silence.

'I'm sorry, Millie,' he said. 'I didn't mean to upset you or anything. I just don't really want to go over there. I want to hang out with Justin and his new mate, Solo. Please forgive me. Pretty please!'

He gave me the irresistible Patrick pleading look and stuck out his bottom lip.

'Fine! Fine! I give in. I forgive you!'

He grinned and leapt over to hug me. There was that tingly feeling again. As soon as his arms made contact with my shoulders I got a shiver down my spine. Though this time, he didn't let go straight away, he kept hugging me and I had this strange glowing feeling that I didn't want him ever to let go.

When he did let go, I smiled and he smiled back as though we both knew what the other had felt, but neither of us said anything. Now wasn't the time to say anything. I didn't want to spoil the moment.

'Hey, Millie! Guess what?' Megan called from the school gate. 'Jason's asked me out again, this Saturday, to a disco at eight. He said Matt already asked you, why didn't you tell us?'

'I completely forgot,' I lied, hoping that Patrick had his ears momentarily closed and hadn't heard anything.

'Who's Matt?' Patrick asked curiously.

I cursed under my breath.

'He's her boyfriend!' Lucinda yelled, a little too loudly.

'No he's not, Luce. I don't even really like him. He's just kind of . . . OK.'

'Then why did you say you'd go to this disco with him?'

'I didn't mean to say yes. It just kind of slipped out.'

Lucinda gave me one of her eyebrow-raising 'yeah, whatever' looks.

'It's true!'

Patrick turned to look at me. 'Why didn't you tell me you had a boyfriend?'

'Umm . . .' I said uneasily. 'Well, I don't know. He's not really all that great, and anyway, he's not my boyfriend. I don't have a boyfriend.'

'So, can I come to this disco?'

'I thought you needed time off from being my friend?'

'Well . . . umm . . . well . . .' he stuttered, 'umm . . . maybe I'd like to go to the disco too. Can I come?'

I nodded. 'Sure – I don't own the place.'

I wasn't sure whether Patrick had really got the right idea about this disco. I could only hope he wasn't expecting me to dump Matt and hang out with him all evening, though why should he think that? I mean, just because I'd been secretly hoping, somewhere in my mixed-up mind, that he might actually fancy me, it didn't mean he was thinking the same thing about me.

Did I want Matt to be my boyfriend? I'd wanted him to be before, I would have given anything to be his girlfriend, but now everything seemed different.

Nothing in my head seemed to make sense. Maybe all the madness with my dad and Abby was what was messing all my thoughts up. I'd become pretty sure I wanted Patrick to be my boyfriend, but I was so scared of losing him as a friend. He was my mate, good old Patrick, the one I could always count on. I could laugh and joke with him, have a good time with him, we could go mad together . . .

Though maybe that would be a good thing to have with a boyfriend too . . .

'Hey, Millie! Can I come to the disco too?' Lucinda asked. 'Please?'

I nodded, having my friends there might make me feel a bit better about going. What if Matt didn't turn up? At least if I was going with others I could still have a good time.

'Can I come too?' Holly asked.

'And me and Danny?' said Kaori, who looked a little happier today.

'Me too?' Jade pleaded.

I nodded again and before I had a chance to speak, everyone was already making arrangements to meet at my house before the disco.

'So, that's agreed. We all meet at Millie's house at seven to get ready. Can you come, Mill?'

I raised my eyebrows at her. It was my house for

goodness' sake! Couldn't I at least have a say in the matter.

I just smiled and the others giggled excitedly. 'God, it's a stupid disco, not the Oscars!' I muttered under my breath.

'What was that, Mill?' Kaori whispered.

I sighed. 'Nothing!'

I got back to Mum's that night and lay on my bed writing my English essay. I wasn't going to go back to Abby's by myself, I just had to hope my lockout plan had succeeded, the builders had come and gone and the taps were unfitted.

Yes, now I could relax . . . easy. So why was I finding that so hard?

Chapter 10

Q is for Questioning and R is for Raining in my head

Beep! Beep! Beep! Beep! Beep! Bee . . .

I hit the clock radio extra hard in some hope that I'd murder it in the process. Why did it have to sing so early? My head was ringing, my nose was running and my chest was pumping.

'Mum! I feel awful! Can I stay home today?'

This was a bad move. Mum had been up extra early that morning with Josh and she wasn't in a very good mood.

Mum put her hands on her hips and growled disapprovingly.

'This was sudden. Got any tests today?'

I shook my head. I then held it tightly.

'Oh, for goodness' sake, Millie! You're going to school and that's final!'

I sulked, but it hurt my head too much. Why couldn't my mum just accept the fact that I'm allowed to be ill sometimes? Why should her bad mood darken my day?

I stumbled downstairs and my headache was just

beginning to fade a little when the phone started to ring. I winced.

'Millie, could you get that, please? I'm busy with Josh!'

I rolled my eyes.

'Can't Rachel get it?'

'Just get the phone, Mill!' I heard Rachel call from behind her door. 'I'm having a serious bad hair day!'

I sighed and headed over to the phone.

'Hello?' I groaned into the receiver.

'Hi, Mill! It's Dad here. I tried to call you yesterday, but the phone was engaged and your mobile was off. Well, anyway, even though we went all the way to the builders and the kitchen shop on Sunday . . . apparently the key wasn't there when the builders arrived. Did they call to ask? No! They just left and they're now fully booked up until . . . well. They can't come out for ages so it seems that Abby can't move back for a while. And now that the key's missing, she's really worried about burglars while she's away. I'm going to have to go and have the locks changed for her. I just don't understand where that key could have gone.'

The smile growing on my face and my headache disappearing seemed to happen simultaneously. She can't move back in for a while! More time with Dad! I did a small dance in the hall and watched as my sister shuffled past in disgust. I stuck my tongue out at her. I can dance if I want to.

I sighed. 'Oh, right.'

'Her sister, Glenda, is having her husband's parents over. Abby was meant to be staying there a few weeks, but apparently Glenda's mother-in-law has done something to her hip and so has to come and stay. I've invited Abby to stay at mine instead, which means she'll be coming this weekend and staying for a while. That OK, Mill?'

My face dropped twenty thousand feet and my headache bounced back.

'Yeah, well, I've got to go, Dad. See you!'

I dropped the phone back on the hook and held my head. Fantastic! Fan-blooming-tastic!

I trudged out of the door, head hung low, mind in a state of confusion. Why had I even thought that my plan would work? As if anything in my life could ever run according to plan!

I pulled a Paracetamol capsule out of my coat pocket and rammed it down my throat in the hope it would make me feel better, and headed to school.

'Are you OK? You don't look well. Should you be in school?' I heard Patrick shout from the gate.

I sighed. 'You know as well as I do that unless I'm bleeding to death, my mum won't dream of letting me stay off school.'

'So, what's up?'

'What do you mean? Why does something have to be up?'

'Because I know you and I know that the face

you've got on is not an "I'm ill" face, it's a "something's upset me" face!'

'Well, it's the plan.'

'What plan?'

I thumped him, hard, right in the stomach.

'What was that for?'

I rolled my eyes. 'I'm not in the mood for your teasing today, Patrick! I'm really not!'

'Well, what about the plan, then?'

I sighed and put my right arm over his shoulder.

'Well, it completely backfired. Taking the key was meant to keep her at her sister's for longer. I thought it was a foolproof plan.'

'So what happened?'

'Well, it started just as I wanted it to. The builders couldn't get in, they left and now they're all booked up for weeks and can't come back out. But Abby's sister is having people over to stay so there's no room for Abby!'

'Isn't that even better? Doesn't that mean that she'll have to stay even further away?'

'No, dufus! It means that my dad's invited her to stay with him. She's going to be *living* under the same roof as me, sleeping in the same bed as Dad.'

Patrick wrinkled his nose. 'So what do we do now, Mill?'

I sighed. 'There's only one thing we can do, Pat.'

'What?'

'Bring her down!'

'Umm . . . is that really such a good idea?'

'Of course it is. All we have to do is show my dad the photograph of her with that other man and tell him about the phone call.'

'How can you get him to know about those things without admitting you were in her house?'

'Umm . . . I can say I found the picture in our house. She could have left it there or something.'

'And the phone call?'

'I guess . . . I guess I can't tell him about that. But hopefully the photo should be enough.'

'Enough for what?'

'Enough to get him to see her for what she is.'

'But won't that break them up?'

I grinned. 'You bet!'

'Umm . . . I dunno if that's such a good idea, Millie. I mean, you can't mess with people's emotions like that.'

'But he has to know!'

'Won't it break his heart?'

'No! He still has me, doesn't he?'

Then, for a moment I wondered how Dad *would* react . . .

'Want a peanut?'

I greedily took one from the blue packet he was offering me.

'Yuck, Patrick. What the hell have you done to them?'

'Just given them a bit of flavour!'

'With what?'

'Marmite, of course!'

'Oh my god, Millie! Are you OK?' Lucinda called as she wandered through the gate. 'You look awful! Will you be OK for Saturday?'

I sighed to myself. I had no idea, I was just so confused. A gorgeous dream boy had asked me to a disco and I might not be able to go because of my cold. Drat it all!

But then again, maybe that was a good thing. I didn't even know if I wanted to face him. I mean, I really liked Matt, but I hardly knew him. How could I be in love with someone I knew nothing about?

And Patrick . . .

How did I feel about both of them being there?

Chapter 11

S is for Silly old me!

So after school I headed over to Dad's to show him the photograph. I rubbed my hands together eagerly. In about two hours I would be free of Abby altogether. Never to see her again and it would be me and Dad, just me and Dad, like it always was. Then, he'd take me out again, he'd love me again! I smiled to myself all the way there, just thinking of the future made me glow inside.

When I reached the house, I could hear the shouting before I even entered the road. Dad was yelling at Mr Goggle for chewing up his slippers (again). I could tell straight away. I've known him since birth, after all.

'Oh, hi Millie! You're a sight for sore eyes! Could you perhaps tempt Mr Goggle into the kitchen with a piece of something?'

I stared down at his left foot to see a scraggy dog attached to it. It was growling menacingly. The term 'ravenous wolf' came to mind.

I sighed. 'Sure,' I said, and ran to the kitchen to get

a slice of ham from the fridge. 'Be back in a moment!'

After getting the mutt off my dad's slipper and into the safety of the (locked) kitchen, I decided it was time to confront Dad about the photograph while Abby was nowhere to be seen. Oh, just my luck because as I was about to whip the shiny paper from my trouser pocket, guess who happened to open the door? Yep, the slimy sea witch herself.

'Hiya, darling!' she called, dropping her shopping and putting her arms around my dad's neck. 'Good day?'

My dad grinned, they kissed, I threw up (well not literally).

'Look!' I yelled, pulling the crumpled photo out of my trouser pocket. 'Look at this!'

Dad stared at the shiny paper in an attempt to see what in the name of overweight poodles he was supposed to be looking at.

'Abby. What is the meaning of this?' he said sternly, handing Abby the photograph.

'Where did you get this? You've been through my stuff!' she said.

'Good job too or Dad would never have found out what a two-timing liar you are!'

'Hold on a second! What are you talking about? This is my older brother, Paul.'

My cheeks went pale and for three-and-a-half seconds, I'm sure that my heart stopped altogether.

'Your . . . your . . . your brother?'

She nodded, Dad frowned, and after that, well, I don't really remember anything else. I fainted. It must have been only for about a minute and when I woke up, I had the worst headache in the universe.

Help, I thought to myself. I'm spiralling into oblivion and where did all those stars come from? No, wait, they're not stars. They're men in red coats playing golden trumpets. Ow. My head hurts!

I stumbled my way up the stairs and lay on my bed, face down.

'Millie!' came the voice from behind my closed bedroom door. 'Can I speak with you?'

My stomach turned over and I muttered, 'Come in.'

My dad opened the door and walked towards me. I could almost hear menacing music as he neared. What was he going to do? How was I to know it was her brother? Why was I so silly?

'Are you OK, sweetheart?' Dad smiled softly as he plonked himself on the bed next to me. I nodded.

'Look, when I asked you before if you minded if Abby stayed you said no. That obviously isn't the way you feel, is it?'

I was silent. How could I tell him how I felt? What excuse was there for my behaviour?

'Millie, I know it may be hard for you to accept that I've found someone new, but you have to come to terms with it. I'm with Abby now. Your mum and I split up four years ago.'

I was still silent, totally struck dumb with what an

absolute mess I had made of things.

'Millie! Could you please at least *try* to like Abby! Is that too much to ask?'

I shook my head and let out a long murderous sigh. There was no way in the name of marmite-covered peanuts that I was going to try and like Abby. It's just the same as trying to like being hit on the head with a fifty-stone man and his Land Rover – it's just not possible! She's so annoying, the way she laughs like a hyena, the way she acts like a love-struck teenager when she's really a middle-aged woman – OK, she's in her thirties, but she should still act her age!

'And I want you to know that Abby would never cheat on me, and I would never cheat on Abby!'

I was so angry I couldn't say anything about the phone call. There was no way I could have heard it without being in her house.

'Thanks, Dad!' I sighed, trying my best to look as though I gave a damn about what he'd just said. 'I'd like to be on my own for a bit now if you don't mind.'

He widened his eyes and gave me his 'I don't think so' look. 'Of course, but first I'd like to say how disappointed I am in you, Mill. You know, I don't want you to go to this disco on Saturday.'

My stomach flipped so violently I thought it would fall out altogether. I had to go, even though I may not have wanted to at first. I had to see Matt.

'But Dad! I have to go! I just have to!'

He sighed. 'Well, you're very lucky because even

though I don't want you to go, Abby has persuaded me to let you go.'

I was completely amazed. Abby had told him to let me go?

Dad smiled at the look on my face.

'See? She's not that bad, is she?'

Chapter 12

T is for Terror at the disco

'Holly, do my hair in French plaits, please!'
'Wait your turn, I'm next.'

'Oi, did I say you could use that? Give it back!'

'Millie, can I borrow your blue mini-skirt, I'll be careful!'

'Oops! Damn! Millie, you better get over here!'

Yep, that's the sound of six desperate girls, cramming gallons of make-up on to their faces in my tiny boudoir. Not exactly what I wanted right then. Lucinda had just spilt her Diet Coke all over my new T-shirt, which I may just have been planning to wear, Megan had somehow managed to get nail-varnish just about everywhere *but* her nails and to top it all off, Mr Goggle kept coming in and eating all our munchies when no one was looking.

Luckily my cold seemed to have cleared up, maybe all the excitement had caused it to disappear. I gazed around the manic room and sighed. What the hell was I supposed to wear anyway?

The others hadn't really set a specific dress code.

Megan was in her jeans and black top with 'Bite me' written across the chest in white. Holly was in a very skimpy dress (which, if for some reason she had to bend down, would not only reveal her bum very nicely, but also half her back). It had silver and purple sequins along the bottom and was made of some kind of purple silk.

Jade was in a long flowing blue skirt which ran almost down to her black velvet sandals. On the top she had a white blouse and an awful lot of jewellery on her arms. To be brutally honest, it looked more like she was going to a Hippy Chick's fancy dress party than to a disco.

Kaori had spent most of the time in the bathroom – we assume getting herself into top form, ready for Danny, but that can be quite annoying when you're busting for the bog and the only other toilet within walking distance is the old wood shed at the bottom of our garden.

Lucinda had a bright orange V-neck top with 'Whahoo' in red letters sprayed across the centre, black fishnet tights with mini badges all over, a short yellow skirt, maybe shorter than Holly's dress, and big chunky sandals with platforms three feet high. It was very scary, but actually looked really good.

Anyway, Holly was in charge of hair and make-up and it wasn't long before all the girls, minus me and Kaori, were queuing up for her level of expertise. By this time it was half an hour before take-off and I was still sitting on my bed in my pyjamas.

I didn't know what to wear. I mean, what could I wear that would completely wow Patrick and make him fall completely in love with me?

Did I just say Patrick? I meant Matt, didn't I? Maybe I didn't, maybe I meant Patrick.

'Millie, you have to get ready!' Holly called, plaiting Lucinda's orange hair. 'Hurry up, what are you wearing?'

I sighed. 'I really have no idea! Help me, Hollz!'

She smiled and turned towards my wardrobe.

'Right, what have we got?'

In the end I found myself dressed in my glitter covered jeans and shimmery halter-neck top. Holly's eyes scanned me and she smiled madly.

'There we go, you look gorgeous!'

'Thank you, Hollz! How can I ever thank you?'

She shrugged. 'What are friends for?'

'Time to go!' Dad called from downstairs.

'Kaori!' I yelled. 'Let's go!'

'I feel kind of sick,' came the reply. 'Go, I'll hang here!'

'What?' I shouted back. 'You can't just stay here! Come on, it'll be fun!'

'No, I really don't want to!' she yelled.

'What about Danny?'

'If you see him there, then just tell him I'm ill.'

'Shouldn't you call him?'

There was no reply.

The other girls looked at me puzzled, I shrugged

109

at them, I had no idea what to do, I couldn't make
her go.

'Umm . . . OK, Kaz. Won't be the same without
you!'

We all thundered downstairs and grabbed our
coats.

'Where's Kaori?' my dad questioned.

'She's not coming, she doesn't feel very good.'

Abby came out of the living room and smiled at us
all. 'Why doesn't she come and watch the TV with
me while you're all out?'

My dad grinned. 'Great idea. Have fun!'

He kissed Abby goodbye and we all piled into my
dad's big people carrier.

'Hey Mill, this is fab, isn't it?' Holly yelled over the
booming music. 'Which one's Matt?'

I hadn't seen him in the whole two-and-a-half
minutes we'd been in the sweaty hall. I was
beginning to think that maybe he wasn't going to
come.

'I bet he doesn't exist!' Lucinda shouted in mid-
dance move.

'He does!' I yelled back.

'What?' the girls yelled.

I shook my head as though to say it didn't matter.

A finger poked me on the shoulder and I turned
round.

'Where's Kaori?' Danny asked.

'Not coming,' I shouted back over the music. 'She wasn't feeling too good.'

'Well, that's *great*!' he said unsympathetically. 'I guess I'll go, then. She could have told me.'

I rolled my eyes at him as he pushed his way through the crowd. It was hardly Kaori's fault if she was ill. Surely he should understand? What an idiot.

'Oh shit!' I mouthed as the gorgeous blond-haired boy wandered in with his skateboarding mates. 'Oh shit and triple shit!'

Holly spun round and whispered in my ear. 'Which one's Matt?'

At first I couldn't tell, but I had a tummy turning feeling that he was the one heading my way.

'Want to dance?' he said, grinning at me.

I took his hand and we headed out onto the dance floor, our faces lit by the revolving disco ball. Spotlights went crazy with the music and we danced together, bodies touching. I had to keep pinching myself, it just didn't seem to be real. I was dancing with the sexiest boy in the room! Matt was dancing with me! He was with me!

But where was Patrick?

I watched a group of really attractive blonde girls wander past, eyeing Matt up, I held him closer, he was mine! I looked at him, and him at me, our eyes connected. I couldn't help looking at his lips, what would it be like to kiss them?

Then it happened, we were dancing away and our

lips met, his soft kiss tingling all the way down my spine. I was in heaven at that moment and I felt like nothing could knock me back down.

I felt one of his hands running down my back and round my body. At first it was strange, it was a new experience for me and I wasn't sure if I liked it or not. Then it was *too* strange. Too fast. I just didn't feel comfortable any more. I tried pushing the wriggling hands away, but they persisted.

'Can you stop?' I asked.

But he didn't stop, whether he'd heard me or not, I wasn't sure.

'Get off!' I finally yelled. 'Get off!'

Then out of the blue, a knight in shining armour came to my rescue. He strolled over to Matt with power in his stride and yelled, 'You leave her alone!'

'Or what?' Matt mocked. 'Are you going to hit me?'

And he did! He gave Matt a right old punch.

I watched as Matt's hand wandered up to his face and he felt the area the fist had landed on. People around us had stopped dancing and were staring at Matt as he walked closer to my rescuer.

He aimed a punch right at his head.

'Patrick!' I yelled.

Patrick. The same Patrick that used to push me in the swimming pool when we were ten, used to throw water balloons at me and even rugby tackled me in public, the very same one!

I couldn't believe it. Who else would have done that for me? Who else would have protected me like that?

As soon as I saw Matt's angry fist heading towards Patrick's head I knew which one I wanted as a boyfriend. The fear for Patrick's safety took over everything and my stomach was knotted so tightly I felt like I couldn't breathe.

I think the music stopped just before the impact, but it felt like it happened the same time.

We were thrown out of the disco for it. One of the people supervising came over and broke it up. I think it was over then, anyway.

So Holly, Megan, Jade, Lucinda, Patrick and I headed out of the disco and I called my dad who wasn't too happy about leaving the pub early, but he came anyway. Which is lucky because who knows how we would have got home otherwise. I was really worried he'd get Abby to pick me up, but I suppose after the whole photograph misunderstanding, he knew better.

We all stumbled into the people carrier explaining how the disco had been really boring and we just couldn't stick it any longer. I have no idea what my dad would have said if he'd known the truth. He certainly wouldn't have let me go to another disco until I was, like, fifty-two. Luckily he hadn't noticed Patrick's face.

I positioned myself next to Patrick in the car and

stared at the bruise developing on the side of his face. It made me smile, the memory of him standing up for me like no one ever had before, like I doubted no one else ever would. And I then knew that he was what I wanted more than anything. He was the one for me.

As Dad swerved his way round a corner I felt my knee bump into Patrick's, which created a shiver that was so warm and magical it made me feel . . . complete in a way, because I finally knew what I wanted.

I lifted my gaze from the floor up to Patrick's face. He was looking at me with his amazing Patrick smile and so I smiled back at him. I giggled inside as his little finger slid over mine.

So even though it was a short evening of madness, it was a good evening, because it made my feelings for Patrick that much clearer. He'd saved me! He'd taken that punch for me.

When we got back, Kaori wasn't around. She'd obviously got sick of our house and headed back to hers.

So my dad drove my friends back to their own houses and I headed upstairs to bed. Though, once up there, I didn't feel tired any more. My gaze floated over to the mobile phone on the desk.

I scrolled through the phonebook and hit the call button.

'Hey, Kaori, are you OK?'

There was nothing but a trail of sniffing from the other end.

'Why didn't you want to go to the disco? Were you really sick?'

She sniffed. 'No!'

'I thought as much. What's up? It's not like you to lock yourself in the bathroom for ages. Is it your dad?'

'I think she knows!'

'Who? Who knows what?'

'My mum! I think she's found out that my dad's having an affair.'

'Oh,' I sighed, finally waking up from whatever sleep I'd been in. Poor Kaori. I was out partying at the disco, having a good time, feeling on top of the world because of Patrick and she was drowning in tears. Her parents might be getting divorced and I was stressing about my dad's girlfriend.

'Why didn't you say anything earlier?'

'Everyone was there. I don't want everyone to know.'

'I guess I can understand that. So what happened?'

'Well, they were arguing yesterday and I'm sure it was about that! What if they get divorced, Mill? I don't know if I could handle that. I'm not as strong as you!'

I smiled at the irony to myself. She had it wrong. I *wasn't* strong – I had coped with it, but I'd simply hidden all my feelings from people. I guess I was a bit of a coward, I hoped that if I ignored it, it would go away or something.

'Are you sure that's what they were arguing about?'

'Yeah! My mum kept mentioning Vanessa, and did Vanessa know this . . . blah blah! I mean, she'll leave him, won't she? Who would stay with their husband if they were cheating on them?'

And then it hit me! That's what I had to do! I had to get it to look like my dad was seeing someone else and then Abby would leave! It was so simple, why hadn't I seen it before?

'Oh my God, Kaz! I've got the perfect plan for my dad! I can get him to look like he's seeing someone else and Abby will leave! It's a sure thing!'

There was only furious sobbing on the other end. I knew as soon as I heard it that I'd been stupid and said the wrong thing.

'Millie! Is that all you ever think about? Yourself and your plan? I'm here, telling you how awful it is. I hear my mum crying and I know it's because she knows about the affair, it's breaking her heart and you want to impose that on someone? On your dad's girlfriend? When it's not even true?'

'Kaori, I'm so . . .'

And the phone went dead. I sighed to myself. How could I have been so insensitive? Kaori was feeling awful and I'd made her feel worse. What sort of a friend would do that?

And what about what she'd said? Well, they're not married – Dad and Abby haven't been going out a long time. It wasn't exactly the same, they'd get over it. People two-time all the time. People get dumped all the time. They'd get over it, wouldn't they? They'd be fine.

Chapter 13

U is for Undercover

Waking up on Sunday morning was not too wonderful. My mouth was dry and sticky, my head was pounding and I had a dog on the bed beside me licking my face. I solved problem three by pushing Mr Goggle on to the floor. Problem one was taken care of by the glass of water beside me; there was nothing I could do to help my head. It wasn't a headache that could be magically fixed by a tablet or a spoonful of medicine. The pain pulsing round my brain was due to the many problems spinning in my mind.

Why did Patrick have to be visiting family today? I needed to see him.

Was Kaori right about my plan for Abby?

Stupid question, I knew she was. I knew how wrong and cruel it was to do that to someone, I knew I shouldn't even be thinking about it.

I sighed.

Was getting my dad back worth breaking Abby's heart?

Well, she was ruining our father-daughter relationship. He was going to move away with her. It was going to change everything!

And she'd get over it, wouldn't she? Yes, Abby would most certainly be upset for a day or two, but she'd be fine. And Dad? He'd be fine too, and he'd be back to his old self in no time whatsoever.

So, I set about thinking, pacing round the room, just waiting for an idea to come to me. I turned my music on, and then off again, and then back on, and off. I fiddled my fingers, I brushed my hair, I paced. I tapped my fingers on the wall, I watched myself in the mirror, I paced.

I picked up my mobile, thinking of calling or texting someone. Maybe they could come up with something, but I didn't want to act out someone else's idea. I wanted to formulate my own.

Isn't it strange how ideas come to you just when you've given up all hope of actually thinking of one? I spent over an hour just pacing round my room, thinking of countless plans, reminding myself of every film I'd seen, every book I'd read. But they were all too complicated, impossible, too small, too big and, when I finally decided to call it a day, it hit me.

I was brushing my hair, watching myself in the mirror as the brush slid through and my eyes darted towards my desk. There, perched on the end next to a pile of school books, was the plan. That's when the light bulb flicked on in my head.

That was *it*!

I practically threw the hair brush down on the floor as I turned myself to face the desk. I picked up the tiny yellow bottle and smiled. It was a start, that's what it was. It was the start, the beginning of the mission.

I wandered downstairs and sat in front of the television, I can't even remember what was on. I was too busy waiting, just waiting for the opportune moment.

Dad and Abby were sitting in the kitchen behind me, quietly talking about nothing in particular. I was half listening to them. I listened for almost half an hour before I finally heard what I was hoping for.

'Right, I'm off out,' said Abby. 'I should be back in . . . oh, umm . . . about an hour or so.'

I turned to look behind into the kitchen and I watched Abby pick up a few bags and slowly leave the house. The door slammed shut behind her.

This was it.

I took a deep breath and squeezed the small glass bottle in my sweaty palm.

I waited for Dad to make his way into the study before I went anywhere. From his position in the kitchen he would have no trouble seeing exactly what I was doing. I didn't want that. I definitely didn't want that.

So once he was out of sight, I got up from the sofa and wandered into the hall. Dad's coat lay swinging on its hook by the door. I smiled at it.

The unopened bottle of perfume was clutched in my hand, the coat was right in front of me. Here was my chance, so why wasn't I taking it?

Wasn't I being spoilt? Wasn't it selfish to do this? Was I doing it for Dad, or for myself? If I did this, if I put perfume on his coat, Abby's suspicions would be roused. She would wonder about it, she would question him about it and when Dad couldn't come up with any answers, would she believe he didn't know how it got there? What would Dad think if there was mystery perfume on his jacket? Would he assume it to be Abby's?

Whatever the outcome may be, I was going to have to try it. It didn't matter who I was doing it for. The fact was, I was doing it! I couldn't walk away now. I couldn't put all the plans to rest and let Dad and Abby move to a far away location without me. I couldn't let myself be replaced.

I took the lid off the perfume bottle and dabbed it round the collar of Dad's coat. Not too little, not too much. I thought about lipstick on the collar, but decided against it. I didn't want to do too much. I could use lipstick later if it was needed.

So I grabbed my coat, slung it over my shoulders and shouted, 'I'm going out, Dad. I'll see you later!'

I waited for a reply, but there wasn't one, so I opened the door and walked round the corner. There I waited for Abby's return.

It was cold, it was damp, it was more than a bit miserable, but I waited round the corner all the same. I waited for Abby to get home from town, then I could come back from 'my friend's house' and watch her as she put everything together in her mind, watch her as she grew sick with . . .

I told myself not to think about how Abby would feel. It didn't matter, only the happily ever after mattered.

So I waited there until I saw the red car pull up outside, and Abby step out of the driver's seat. I watched as she went round to the boot of the car and removed half a dozen carrier bags from it.

Then I moved, I came round the corner and she gave me half a smile when I came into her sight.

'Hi, Millie, what've you been up to?'

I wandered up to the front door and turned round to face her. 'Just been to Holly's house,' I said.

She smiled faintly and walked towards me and the door, carrying her shopping bags.

I took a deep breath as I opened the door, I could faintly smell the perfume as I came in, but maybe that was because I knew it was there. I don't think Abby had noticed it at that point because she didn't seem to smell anything at first.

I watched as she headed over to the coat hooks. I watched her nose wrinkle as she removed her coat and hung it on one of the empty hooks behind the door. Her nose wrinkled a second time, and then a third.

The fourth one made me feel guilty and the fifth one – the fifth one made me feel awful because this time it wasn't just a simple 'what's that smell?' wrinkle of the nose, her eyes showed curiosity, almost suspicion.

'Come over here, do you smell that?' she asked me.

I took a deep breath and nodded. 'Yes, I smell it.'

'Is it yours?'

I just shook my head, and with this one simple head movement, Abby's eyes darkened.

I didn't want to stand there with her – that would be a sign that I knew something, wouldn't it? Normally when I come through the door I head straight up the stairs without a thought. This time I hadn't, this time I'd stuck around, but I'd stuck around long enough.

I hurried up the stairs and turned to go into my room, but something stopped me. I paused outside for a moment and turned round. I looked back to the stairs.

What was the point of setting up an amazing plan if you're not even going to view the results. So I positioned myself at the top of the stairs, cleverly concealed by the small bookcase on the landing, and watched.

At first I couldn't see her, though after a second or two I noticed the legs. They were coming out from underneath the perfumed coat. At first I thought she was just smelling the fabric, to see if that was indeed where the perfume was coming from. Though half a second more gave me the truth.

She was crying.

She was crying because of me.

I'd made her cry.

I felt guilty, of course I felt guilty, and a part of my mind was telling me to come out from my hiding place and tell her I'd done it and not to worry. Instead, I got up, walked into my bedroom and shut the door. I was thinking about the second stage and what I would do to her then.

I heard the argument later. Mind you, they were shouting so loudly you would have to be completely deaf not to hear.

'No Abby, I'm not, I promise you!' my dad said loudly. He wasn't shouting, just speaking strongly.

'Well, how do you explain the perfume on your coat?' Abby shouted, she was crying, I could tell.

'What perfume?'

'There's perfume on your coat!' she screamed.

'Well, it's obviously yours, isn't it?' Dad said calmly.

'I think I would know my own perfume when I smell it!'

'Calm down, calm down!'

'Don't tell me to calm down! You're seeing another woman and you're telling me to calm down.'

'Abby, I'm *not* seeing anyone else.'

'Well, that perfume got on your coat somehow!'

'Well, I have no idea how it got there!' Dad was losing his patience now, his voice was rising into a shout.

'Not good enough!' she screamed.

I heard loud stamping footsteps, followed by a slamming door.

'Abby!' my dad called pointlessly. 'Don't go!'

But she was already out the door, and she didn't come back for a few hours.

When she did, there was no shouting, all I could hear from my room was, 'I'm so sorry' from both parties.

When I woke up on Monday I half-smiled to myself. The ball was rolling, suspicion had been sparked, I was on my way to getting my dad back. I had the second stage all ready. I reached under my bed for something with my dad's handwriting on. I found an old letter he'd written for school and traced the letters I needed through on to a Post-it Note. *Vanessa – 029 20548293, 7:00, Antonio's Pizzeria.*

This would be the final stage of my plan, the plan that couldn't possibly fail.

I snapped out of my grinning moment when the phone rang.

'I'll get it Dad,' I yelled as I thundered down the stairs and into the hall.

'Hello?'

'Hi, Mill! It's me!'

'My knight in shining armour!' I giggled, twirling the cord around my fingers. Once I realised I was doing it I stopped immediately. That's what Rachel always does when she's talking to her boyfriends.

'Yeah,' Patrick mumbled unhappily, 'about that, I'm sorry and everything. I didn't mean to get carried away or anything. You see it was just . . . and I thought . . . what I mean is . . .'

'Could you translate, please? In case you hadn't noticed, I'm not fluent in Patrick!'

'Well, I'm just sorry, OK?'

'Patrick, you have nothing to feel sorry *for*. It's not your fault. You saved me from that slime-ball!'

There was no response from the other end.

'Patrick, is everything OK? You don't sound right.'

I listened for a response, but all I could hear was some strange pop singer wailing in the background.

'I'm . . . I'm . . . I'm fine. See you!'

Then he hung up, leaving me in the hallway stunned and speechless, holding a dead phone in my right hand.

'Millie! The bus is coming round the corner!' Dad yelled from downstairs. I ignored him. Doesn't he know I don't catch the bus any more?

I bolted out the door carrying my coat and bag in an attempt to catch up with Patrick who had nicely decided not to wait at the bus stop this morning.

'Patrick!' I yelled. 'Patrick!'

He turned round and I gave him a knowing glance.

'What's the rush? Didn't have time to stop and wait for your old pal Millie?'

He sighed. 'That's not it, I just . . . sort of forgot!'

I didn't argue the point that he'd never forgotten before in the seven years we'd been walking to school together, or the fact that he has the best memory in the entire world. I just kept quiet the rest of the way. It was clear to anyone with half an eye that Patrick was most definitely *not* in the best of moods.

'Millie, are you OK, you know, after Saturday?'

'Millie, are you feeling all right?'

'Millie, how are you?'

After the seven hundred and fifty-second time someone asked me 'how I was feeling' I was feeling seven hundred and fifty-two times worse than I was when I came in.

'Where's Kaori?' I asked, puzzled. 'I haven't seen her since before the disco.'

Neither had anyone else, in fact. I sighed, I'd done a royal job of killing her will to go on, hadn't I?

After an exhausting day in stupid school, I headed home alone.

My next idea came when my eyes landed on the phone box. Surely an anonymous phone call would arouse further suspicion. I knew Abby had every other Monday and Tuesday off work. The art shop had extra staff working so Abby took the days off.

I checked my pockets for change, and headed into the box. I slipped the coin into the slot and dialled the number of my dad's house. I waited for it to start ringing.

After three or four rings Abby picked up the phone and said, half-cheerily, 'Hello?'

I put the phone back on the hook and smiled. Should I do it again? No, a girlfriend of Dad's wouldn't call again straight away, once was enough.

I sat down on the grass in South Gate Park and stared at the almost black sky in awe and admiration. It was so cold, yet I didn't mind at all. Then I felt it, this cold tingle up my spine, followed by a warm glow in my tummy. I couldn't stop smiling. It had to be him, right? Only soulmates have that effect on you.

'Millie! I'm sorry!'

'Look, if those words pass through your lips again, then I shall have to shoot you!'

Patrick twiddled his fingers. 'Can I sit here?'

'Sure, pull up some grass!'

'Look,' he said slowly as he sat down beside me in the field. 'I wanted to give you this.'

I turned to look at his smooth skin and perfect freckles and then down at his cupped hands. There, neatly sitting in the groove of his palm, was the sweetest thing in the whole world, well, to me anyway. Three single daisies tied together in the smallest, most fragile ring I'd ever seen. So fiddly, but so effective.

'It's really hard to find these at this time of year, but I know how much you like them.'

I brought my hand to my mouth as Patrick gently eased the daisies on to my ring finger. Then I felt the shiver again, the one that only a few weeks ago had scared and confused me, but now was making me feel the absolute best that I'd ever felt, making me feel like someone special.

I giggled and he smiled, leaving me with the feeling that I never wanted to go. I could've stayed in that field until the cows came home.

'Millie,' he sighed thoughtfully, brushing the wisp of hair in front of my eyes aside. 'I think I'm in love with you!'

There, he'd said it, exactly what I'd wanted him to say in exactly the way I wanted him to say it. Then he leaned over me and kissed me, so lightly that I wasn't even sure it was happening at first. That soft caress was everything I'd dreamed of and more.

As soon as his lips touched mine I was whisked away – I don't even know where, to a paradise island with coconuts and strawberry cocktails! I can't remember when it ended because I was feeling it all the way home and singing to myself, sweet melodies that I didn't even know I knew.

I was back at my dad's because Mum and DM were out at a party late. I was so high I hardly noticed Dad and Abby with their arms round each other on the sofa. I just twirled all the way up the stairs and into my bedroom. Wow!

*   *   *

The next morning I had this surreal feeling that the whole thing had been my imagination, but there it was, that daisy ring, rubbing against my finger as living proof. It wasn't half as beautiful as it had been yesterday, the delicate, once-white petals were more a dismal brown. It didn't really matter to me, though. I took it off and popped it in the drawer of my desk with care so that it wouldn't fall off or get damaged.

Nothing could bring me out of my romantic state, not the thought of school, not the couple in the kitchen staring into each other's eyes lovingly. Nothing seemed to bother me really.

I had to hit myself over the head with a cushion a few times to try and get the melodic fantasy out of my silly little mind. I had to think about other things, like going to school and working on getting rid of Abby. I had so many ideas to create the impression of another woman, I just didn't know where to start.

Once I had gained a bit more control over the vision of last night's romantic (ish) encounter, I headed to school. Absolutely the last place I wanted to be at any time, but certainly on this specific Tuesday when most probably every person I ran into would be asking me what the smile on my grinning face was all about. I wasn't going to tell them about what had happened and I was hoping and praying Patrick would have the sense to do the same. Was it their business? Absolutely not!

'Camilla, did you want this?' Abby called from the

doorstep, handing me a black coat.

I smiled back at her and took it from her hand. I decided not to wait for Patrick. To be completely honest, I was kind of scared of seeing him. I wanted it to be real. What if I was imagining it? What if it hadn't meant as much to him as it did to me? I'd feel really stupid for wanting to take it further if he didn't. I didn't want to wake myself from the daydream. I mean, had it really happened? Would he bring it up? What would I say to him if he did? Oh yeah, this thing was supposed to be out of my mind.

'Millie! Where were you after school yesterday? I was trying to phone you!' Lucinda yelled at me before I'd even got through the school gate. Should I tell them, after all, they were my best mates. No, I couldn't trust them not to burst out laughing and say, 'Patrick? You're not serious?'

I just couldn't trust them.

'Nowhere special. Just . . . down at the park.'

Lucinda shrugged and they all started yapping about something to do with the maths test later (which, I luckily hadn't forgotten about. I'd managed to do all my revision notes last week – maths is actually OK when you get into it). I didn't listen to them, I was too busy thinking about whether Patrick was my boyfriend or not.

Anyway, I rummaged around in my coat pocket for the list of possible ways to pretend Dad was seeing someone else. I had to think of something other than maths, Patrick or daisy rings. This time I wasn't going to hang around for ages, thinking about whether it was the right plan or not. I was going to go for it.

Before the maths test we were all huddled in the corridor by the radiator. Jade was flicking through her exercise book trying to get a bit of last minute revision done. Lucinda was chatting to Megan about last night's *EastEnders* and Megan wasn't really paying much attention at all because her mind was dancing with thoughts of Jason. Holly was staring in her pocket mirror and carefully applying a thin coat of pink sparkly lip-gloss and Kaori was still not in school.

'Millie! How come you didn't wait for me this morning?' Patrick's voice called from behind.

I sighed and turned round to see a very sullen-looking boy.

'Oh, I'm sorry, Pat, it's just well . . . I . . . had to get to school early, for my um . . . cookery project.'

He pulled me away from the others and whispered, 'Are you avoiding me Mill, you know, after last night?'

My stomach lurched as he said the words 'last night'. I hoped he wouldn't say anything, especially in front of the others. I don't know why. I mean, why shouldn't we talk about it? I did enjoy it, I more than enjoyed it, I loved it, for crying out loud! I wasn't embarrassed, was I?

I mean, Patrick certainly wasn't 'sexiest man of the year' material like Matt or Danny, though did that really matter, as long as we had a great laugh together and talked things, through? I mean, an intelligent mate is better than a self-obsessed pretty boy, isn't it? I've never been one of those 'looks are everything' people like a certain Holly I know.

To tell you the absolute truth, until Matt, I'd never really paid that much attention to boys' looks. I've always been one of those personality seekers – though maybe that's because I was only interested in boys as mates. Now I'm on a boyfriend hunt, I don't know what I want any more!

'Were you avoiding me, then?'

I shook my head a few times to remove myself from the wandering daydream I was having and looked back at his freckled face.

'Sorry, Patrick! I didn't mean to avoid you, but yes, in a way I suppose I was!'

'Why? You're not mad, are you?' he asked in a worried voice.

'I don't think so,' I answered honestly. 'I just felt kind of . . . oh I don't know, Patrick. That's my problem . . . I don't know anything at the moment.'

He hugged me and I sighed heavily.

'What's wrong?' he said, removing his arms from my body.

'Can we talk later? Over my house, after school?'

He nodded, but he didn't look particularly happy about it. I guess by the way I'd phrased it, he thought I was going to let him down, but I wasn't. I just had to clear things up with him. Find out where we stood.

* * *

'Millie,' Jade said, smiling as I wandered into the geography room ten minutes late. 'Where've you been?'

'Just talking to people!'

'You'd better watch yourself. The SATs are creeping closer you know – only eight months left. You may have missed something important. Here, you can borrow my book!'

I gave her a raised-eyebrow kind of look as she slid the pristine orange exercise book in my direction.

'Thank you for joining us, Millie!' Mrs Williams announced rather sarcastically. 'As Jade correctly pointed out, you could have missed something very important! Please, settle down and get your book out. The rest of the class is ready to begin.'

'She's listening to our conversations now, is she?' I muttered to smarty-pants Jade as I took my bursting pencil case out.

'I heard that, Millie!'

'See!'

On the way home to my mum's, I decided to call from the phone box again seeing as Abby would probably be there again with her second day off. Patrick had a dentist appointment. He'd left early last lesson and was coming round to my mum's house later, so I walked by myself. I didn't really mind, it gave me time to think, time to breathe.

I had to concentrate on getting Abby to think there was another woman in Dad's life. I didn't know what it would take. How much did Abby trust him? How much did she love him? I just had to keep going, the perfume, the first phone call and now another simple silent call. They always arouse suspicion. Well, they do with me anyway. You pick up the phone and a few seconds later it goes dead. One is a wrong number, two is worrying, and after three, you start to wonder who's after you. Who would want to scare you? Or who wants to talk to someone in the house other than you? Who doesn't want you to know they've called? There's the suspicion and I was hoping a few calls would get her wondering.

I stopped at the phone box near my house and popped a twenty-pence piece into the machine. Then, I dialled the number.

It rang once.

It rang twice.

It rang a third time.

'Hello?' Abby's voice answered.

I waited a second.

I waited another second.

I put the phone back on the hook and sighed.

Should I call again? Or should I leave it a few hours or so?

I decided to leave it. If I was seeing a man and his girlfriend answered, I wouldn't call back straight away. There would be no point, she would answer.

So I stepped out of the phone box and hummed myself home.

Later on, I received a visit from a damp Patrick and his multi-coloured umbrella. I was ready to talk to him – ready to let him know how I felt.

The dripping boy in the porch had a look of his face to match the weather outside.

'Come in!' I said, smiling at him.

He wiped his feet on the slightly mangled, twenty-year-old doormat and stepped inside. I giggled as he shook the equivalent of an entire swimming pool off his sopping umbrella. (It wasn't as funny later though when Mum forced me to clean up the puddle of liquid on my hands and knees, especially when your seventeen-year-old sister is sitting on the stairs laughing her brains out and going, 'You missed a spot!' every two-and-a-half seconds.)

'Look, Patrick,' I said, once in the comfort of my floor-less bedroom (biscuit crumbs and year-old magazines seemed to have become a handy replacement). 'I . . . I . . .'

I didn't finish my sentence, not that that specific sentence actually had an ending. I'd found myself kissing Patrick before I had the chance to think of a reasonable explanation. At first he looked shocked, he had that 'what the hell is happening?' look on his freckled face, but once he got used to it, he found himself kissing me back. I stepped away, leaving him staring at me with his mouth open.

'I guess that's what I wanted to say!' I said, smiling sheepishly.

I felt my cheeks get hotter and hotter, I was blushing and so was Patrick. We spent two hours in my bedroom, just quietly kissing and talking (ratio of kissing to talking 101:3).

So I hadn't actually told Patrick in words how I felt about him, and he hadn't explained to me, but we'd told each other in our own way. When you kiss someone, the way they return a kiss is a signal of how they feel about you. You can tell straight away, it isn't hard.

'Millie!' my mum called from behind the closed bedroom door. 'Can I come in?'

I pushed Patrick away and he pushed me back. We tried not to giggle.

'Yeah.'

Mum wandered in with a crinkled look on her face, which I read as saying, 'What are you two looking so guilty about?'

'I just thought I should remind you about something.'

'Yes? What would that be?'

'Your grandmother's birthday party.'

I turned to look at Patrick and pulled a face at him. He pulled one back.

'When is it?'

She sighed, rolling her eyes. 'Tomorrow, after school!'

Once she was gone, Patrick gave me a 'poor you' kiss. He knows how much my grandmother annoys me. She's not as nice as my mum and she's certainly not one of those fun grandparents. Then he asked me, 'Are we going out now, then?'

I hesitated, I mean, were we? How was I supposed to know? What would my friends say? Would they laugh at me? I could see Holly's face if she found out. She'd be worried I'd forget about her if me and Patrick became an item. Though I spend a lot of time with him now anyway.

I didn't want my friends to think I'd abandon them. I wouldn't – friends always come before boys. There are some unwritten rules you just have to stick to. Though Kaori and Megan seem to be able to have boyfriends and not dump their friends. Maybe it would be OK if they knew.

'Did my mum just say the party was tomorrow?'

Patrick nodded slowly, obviously annoyed I hadn't answered him.

I sighed. 'I was going to sort out more of Abby's plan tomorrow.'

Then I remembered. I was going to go back to the phone box.

'Millie!' I heard a voice call from downstairs. 'It's dinner-time, you'd better send Patrick home.'

I decided to go out after dinner.

I had managed to dodge Patrick's question. I was hoping and praying to God and Buddha (double the chance) that he would forget by the next time I saw him, I knew this was unlikely and with Patrick's mega-memory, that thought was almost as possible as an Eskimo showing up in Africa to buy a pair of sunglasses for his fish.

After eating, I grabbed my coat, told my mum I was going to the shop and headed out the door. It was dark, but it wasn't that cold and it wasn't raining any more.

It only took me about three minutes to get to the phone, but I had to wait ages for the woman before me to finish talking. She kept saying 'goodbye', but didn't actually put the phone down.

Eventually I found myself putting the twenty pence in and dialling the number.

After four rings Abby picked up.

'Hello?'

I said nothing.

'Hello?'

'Hello?'

I put the phone down and shivered. Maybe it was cold after all.

I couldn't sit still all through science the next day. I mean, could you blame me? Patrick was sitting beside me, passing me notes, begging me to tell him my answer, Mr Fletcher was pointing at the board and yattering a load of rubbish, which he insisted we needed in the SATs and I had to go to my grandmother's birthday party in the church hall later and make conversation with a load of million-year-old people. Though I planned to escape from it somehow and try another wonderful idea on Abby. This one was a step up from the last one. But I had something to do at lunch as well . . .

I glanced at the latest note as Patrick passed it to me.

Say something, Camilla!

I had to answer him, didn't I? I mean, it's rude not to reply to someone's notes, especially when they're important questions. I was very tempted to ignore him. Just to turn the other way and pretend that I wasn't being tapped on the arm by a piece of ink-filled paper. I couldn't do that to him though, he was my mate and if I didn't answer him, he wouldn't be for long.

I turned to look at him and I found myself smiling. What was I waiting for?

OK, but in secret. It's no one else's business, is it?

Okey dokey. Yes! Yes! Yes!

I watched Patrick as he did a little comical dance in his chair and stuck his tongue out at the boy next to him.

'I'm glad you find my lesson so amusing, Mr Gordon and Miss Addicott because if you like, you can stay in it all through break time! Would you like me to arrange that for you?'

We shook our heads, but I was still giggling as Patrick took the opportunity to tickle me under the table.

Chapter 14

V is Vanishing from the party of boredom

'Millie!' Jade called from the bench next to the toilets. 'Kaori's really upset about something! She won't come out of the cubicle. Maybe you can get her to come out.'

It had to be the dad thing, didn't it? She'd forced herself to come into school even though she was still upset about it. But, if that's what it was, then I was probably the last person she'd want to talk to about it. I'd upset her with my plans for Abby in a big way.

'Come on, Millie!' Jade yelled, disappearing through the door.

I hurried over, despite my hesitation. I was going to try and help her anyway.

'Kaori!' I called, staring at the three girls waiting patiently by the sinks as Lucinda desperately tried to coax Kaori out with a bar of Dairy Milk chocolate. 'What's wrong?'

I was answered by a series of hiccupy sobs, weeps and boo-hoos.

'We'll leave you to it, then!' Holly said as the bell rang through the room and echoed around the paintless walls.

It looked like I was about to be late for yet another lesson.

'Kaori! What's happened? Is it still about your dad's affair?'

The cubicle door creaked open and Kaori, drenched in tears, shuffled out to meet me.

'Well, no. I'm still upset about that, but . . . but . . . but . . . Danny dumped me!' she cried, wiping her dripping eyes with the huge roll of loo paper she was holding.

'Oh, Kaori!' I sighed sympathetically.

Poor girl, everything seemed to be collapsing around her, her world turning to dust.

'I just saw him . . . him . . . kissing Marisol outside . . . the . . . the . . . maths . . . room. I thought he loved me,' she snorted. 'I thought he was special!'

I reached over and gave her a reassuring hug. She was in an awful state.

'I couldn't get the vision of them kissing out of my mind. It's still there! I mean, he didn't even apologise! I went over to have a row with him and he just said, "You're dumped." When I asked him why, he said that he was tired of waiting for me to be ready . . . you know . . . to go all the way.'

She burst into tears again and wiped her running nose on my shoulder. I tried not to mind.

'And now I don't have a boyfriend, what am I going to do?'

'Why do you have to have a boyfriend, Kaz? It's not like you *need* one, is it? At least not right now. I don't think you'll have to wait long for someone else.'

She sniffed and wiped her nose on another piece of toilet paper.

'Anyway, you're so busy at the moment with your next gymnastic competition coming up. And you've got me, and the others. You can spend more time with us now.'

Kaori didn't look convinced.

'There'll be other boys, they come and go all the time. Your friends will always be here for you, no matter what. We all love you to bits. Who needs boys, anyway?'

'I do need a boyfriend, Mill!'

'But why?'

'Because . . .'

She wiped her eyes with the tissue she was holding and looked up at me.

'Oh, I don't know, having someone there makes me feel more attractive.'

'You don't need a boyfriend to be attractive, Kaz! You're the most attractive person I know. You're completely gorgeous. Some people would give their life savings to look like you.'

'Doesn't mean I don't feel insecure sometimes.'

I hugged her again and looked at my watch discreetly so that Kazza wouldn't be offended. We were ten minutes late already.

'Are you feeling up to English?' I asked her, in the hope she'd smile and nod happily and we wouldn't get too much of a yelling from Mr Henderson. She blew her nose and cried again, a long wailing cry that echoed through the empty toilets. I took it as a 'no way'.

'Well, I'll take you down to reception and say you're ill, yeah?'

She nodded.

After I'd taken the sobbing Kaori to her ticket home, I arrived in English twenty five minutes late.

'Where have you been, Millie?' Mr Henderson yelled as I wandered through the door.

'She was skipping class, sir!' Louis yelled. I stuck my middle finger up at him while Mr Henderson wasn't looking.

'I was taking my friend down to reception. She wasn't . . . umm . . . very well.'

'Liar!' Louis's voice shouted.

'Well, do you have a late slip?'

I pulled the crumpled paper from my pocket and handed it to him with a half-smirk on my face, then I went to sit next to Holly and Jade.

'What did she say?' Holly whispered.

'Nothing.'

'That was a long time for her just to say nothing.'

'Copy this from the board and *no* talking!' Mr Henderson bellowed in our direction.

After an English lesson from hell – involving silence, boredom and menacing glares from Mr Henderson – I got on the bus and tried to psyche myself up for the extra boredom of the party ahead. I mean, did it even deserve the title 'party'? Parties are supposed to involve loud music and bopping till you're dropping, not tea and biscuits while listening to Mozart and conversations about the weather.

Once there ('there' being the smelly dark hall of the local church) I sat myself down and helped myself to a can of Coke from the buffet table. My eyes spent ninety-two percent of the time firmly fixed to the watch on my wrist. It was four o'clock, and at precisely six o'clock Abby would be returning from her little art shop. I had to slip away quietly for half an hour to lay out the plan and wait in the bushes across the road to, hopefully, see her emerge in a flood of tears. It was dodgy – I could be caught at any time, but let's face it – I had to do it, I didn't have much of a choice.

'You couldn't pass me one of those delicious looking cream cakes, could you, Millie love?' my tubby Uncle Harry said, rubbing his ever-expanding waistline with his pudgy hand.

I passed him the cakes and watched in amazement as he transferred every last eclair from the silver serving dish, to his paper plate. Gutsy pig!

4.13 – v. bored

4.14 – duller than dull

4.15 – YAWN!!!!!!!

I stared at the clock and watched the hands tick slowly around the face. It clearly wasn't in a hurry to get anywhere fast – unlike me of course.

After an hour and a half of mooching by the buffet table and passing everyone cakes, biscuits and cucumber sandwiches, I slipped out of the hall quietly to activate my evil plot. Well, I suppose it wasn't technically evil, I mean, I was just trying to spend more time with my dad.

I knew I was cutting it fine, which was why I decided to jog to Dad's. I thanked the Lord it wasn't raining and I didn't even mind the cold. Jogging when it's chilly is a lot better than jogging in warm weather. So the sweaty, red-faced creature (a.k.a. me) headed out in the pitch black night to catch the sea witch.

I jogged past the library with its creepy entrance and graffiti-covered walls, past the park with its swaying swings and dark eerie forest, past the bus stop which in the daytime is a comforting meeting place, but in the dark, is where demons gather and then along the whispering alley where the mumbles you hear are never just the trees talking.

I would be lying if I said I enjoyed my jog, but it would be a bigger lie if I said I wasn't looking

forward to flushing Abby's life down the toilet. I was
. . . I mean, she'd almost certainly ruined mine! She
was going to take my dad away from me. He's the
only dad I have, I didn't want to lose him. I wasn't
going to lose him.

There it was, the regular semi-detached house
that I'd been in and out of for years. A second home
to me, a place I had always trusted to be there, no
matter what. Today it was going to help me kick
Abby out the door. I smiled slightly to myself and
took a deep breath of the cold evening air.

I took shelter in the porch and pulled a handful of
keys out of my coat pocket.

'Here goes!' I said, trembling as I turned the key in
the lock of the door.

The hall had that whole ghostly presence thing
going on, but it seemed to disappear as soon as I
flicked the light switch.

'Spooky!' I muttered to myself. I've always hated
being home alone, although you're never completely
alone when you have a mad terrier around the house.
I tiptoed past Mr Goggle, who was sleeping
peacefully in his basket. What a lazy thing he could
be.

I crept down the dimly-lit corridor and into the
dining room where we keep the phone. It was lighter
there, so I felt safer, warmer, less guilty. I smiled as I
pulled the crumpled piece of paper from my jeans
and laid it by the phone. You see, Dad always writes

notes from his phone calls, he's very forgetful.

There, I'd done it, I'd laid out the plan and still had ten minutes before Abby was due back. I crept back out the house and locked the door, then took my position behind the rose bush across the road.

Chapter 15

W is for Watching and waiting

I sat there, both eyes firmly fixed to the familiar building in front of me. A man carrying a bunch of pink and white flowers walked past, whistling a merry little song, a cyclist wearing a ton of orange and yellow reflective clothing whizzed along, and I must admit, those were the most exciting events while I sat watching and waiting.

Would Mum have realised I was gone? Would she be panicking? Nah, in a crowd like that, who'd miss one person?

Suddenly, there was the loud ringing of a mobile phone. I reached into my pocket and pulled it out. 'Kazza' flashed on the screen.

'Hey, Kaz, are you OK now?'

'Yeh, I think so. I'm better without him anyway.'

'You go, girl!' I said, keeping my eyes on the building in front.

'Anyway, that's not what I called to say.'

'It's not?'

'Nope, my dad isn't having an affair. He never was!'

'Really? Wow, Kaz, that's great!'

'Yeah, the woman I saw him with was his boss. I just saw them in her car, then put two and two together and made five.'

'And what about the arguing?'

'Well, apparently my dad's been going to see this life coach or something who's telling him a load of crap, which he believes. She's called Vanessa, you see.'

'Oh, right!'

'Well, I've got to go, Mill, I have homework to do.'

'Um . . . OK, bye then!'

Just as I put the phone back in my pocket and fixed my eyes on the house again, an unexpected hand landed on my left shoulder. I screamed.

Patrick grinned. 'Hey, it's only me! And, if you don't mind me asking, why are you hiding in a rose bush? Aren't you supposed to be at a party?'

I pulled him down out of view and whispered, 'I am . . . I mean, I was . . . but now I'm not!'

Patrick gave me the 'whatever' look and sat beside me. 'So what *are* you doing in a rose bush at five past six?'

I sighed. 'I'm activating the plan, of course!'

'From a rose bush?'

'Yes, from a rose bush!'

'OK, whatever turns you on.'

'How did you know I was here anyway?'

He smiled and pointed to the house across the road.

'Well, I was up in my room and I saw you hiding.

I was quite confused, so I thought I'd come down here and – '

'Shut up!' I muttered as a red Ford Estate pulled up in front. 'Look, it's her!'

Patrick stood up.

'No! No! Get down, you idiot!'

We crouched low, and watched as Abby stepped out of the driving seat. She opened the boot of the car with one swift hand movement and pulled out a white plastic bag.

'She's in.' I sighed as Abby disappeared into the house. 'Yes! Yes! Yes!'

Patrick turned to look at me, then gave me a puzzled glance – the one where the his forehead crumples and his eyebrows half-cover his eyes like a bulldog.

'I'm not going to ask!' he said, getting up from the floor and starting to head off.

I pulled him back down and hissed, 'She'll be coming out again any minute! Please stay!'

He kissed me gently and smiled, 'Anything for you, Mill!'

I giggled, and we waited for a further ten minutes. Surely she would see the note. I happen to know she always looks by the phone when she gets in, always. After I'd told Patrick not to head home for the millionth time, Abby emerged carrying three black sports bags and her small face was covered in tears, ones I knew I was responsible for.

At that moment, when she turned to look in my

direction, I felt really guilty. I was almost sad to see her like that. What had I done? What had I achieved? I'd ruined her life!

'Millie! You – you – what did you do? Where's she going?'

I said nothing.

'You got her to leave, didn't you?'

I said nothing.

'I think you may have gone too far, Mill.'

I just continued to stare across the road as Abby got into the car.

'I mean, I know you wanted your dad back and everything, but couldn't you have found another way? Couldn't you have tried it for a bit? Seen if she really did change your dad? Seen if he really did spend less time with you?'

'No I couldn't.' I sighed.

'Why not?'

'I know she was changing him. I've known my dad all my life. I know what he was, I know what he is now. And the moving house! I wouldn't see him as much, I know it. I wouldn't see you as much either.'

'But look at her,' Patrick said as a sobbing Abby drove off down the road. 'Was it really worth it? When you think about it, you may not have lost your dad, but *she's* lost him. Just because she loves him in a different way to you doesn't mean she won't hate being without him just as much as you do, maybe even more. Think about that, OK?'

And with that he stood up and headed back into his house. I sat there and stared into the sky, just thinking about what he'd said. Was he right?

Back at the party it was just as exciting as when I left. I mean, the same faces, the same slow music drifting in the background, and Uncle Frank was still totally sloshed as he staggered over to the buffet table for another beer. Thankfully, Auntie May stopped him.

'Millie! Where have you been?' my mum called from across the hall. I rolled my eyes in an attempt to block her out completely, but it failed.

'I don't ask a lot of you, but if you're meant to be somewhere . . . blah blah blah blah blah de blah blah blah . . .'

I watched as her mouth opened and closed and the frown on her face grew bigger and bigger. Practically everyone in the hall was staring at Mum as she waggled her finger at me and turned beetroot-red. Maybe she was slightly annoyed at the fact I'd slipped away from the party. I guess my unnoticeable absence didn't go quite unnoticed.

I sighed to myself. I wasn't in the mood for explaining, I wasn't in the mood for anything. Finally achieving my goal hadn't given me quite the amazing feeling I'd expected it to. It had done quite the opposite. It had completely deflated me.

'So come on, where were you?'

Well, what were the options?

Option A: Tell her the truth (i.e., I had been hiding in a rose bush, watching as my father's girlfriend left in a trail of tears I'd caused).

Option B: Make up a fantastic lie and use my wonderful acting skills to pull it off successfully.

Option C: Avoid the question.

'I'm sorry, Mum! There's no excuse for what I . . .' I spun round to look at Auntie May staring at me in a worrying and crooked way. Was it any of her business? '. . . did. It'll never happen again!'

'Where were you?'

Oh well, seems Option C was an utter failure. Option B, here we come.

'I had to talk to Jade about our homework that's due tomorrow, we're supposed to be working on it together. You see we were going to finish it off today, but I forgot about the party. I thought it wouldn't matter if I popped over to hers for a bit.'

Mum's frown gradually changed into a smile.

'Well, OK, just tell me where you're going next time!'

A round of applause please, I think I've just earned myself an Oscar for Best Liar Ever, I thought.

Mum glanced at her silver watch and sighed exaggeratedly.

'It's almost time to pack up. I want to be home in time for *Star Trek* at nine.'

I nodded, then remembered the look on Abby's face. I tried to convince myself I'd done the right thing. That now I'd have my dad back everything would be OK, everything would be back to normal. But it just didn't seem to stick in my head. Now it was all over I was seeing the whole situation differently. I'd caused Abby great pain, I'd sent her away from the man she loved and now, and now I was feeling sick with guilt.

Patrick had been right, I knew from the moment he said it. Yes, Patrick was right once again and I was wrong. Though it was too late to do anything about it now. Abby was gone.

'I guess you can pop home now if you like,' Mum sighed.

I popped out of my daydream and turned round, assuming she was talking to someone other than me. Though she wasn't, what was up with her? Didn't she want me to suffer by helping her say goodbye to all the half-asleep elders? Didn't she want me to pick up the wooden broom and watch me sweep every speck of gooey and disgusting rubbish from under the tables? Was this a miracle from God?

'Off you go, then, before I change my mind!'

I smiled and grabbed my denim jacket from the coat stand in the corner. She was obviously feeling mucho guilty about yelling at me. What other explanation could there be for her sudden act of kindness?

Walking home along the dimly lit side alley wasn't exactly relaxing. Every rustle, twitch and snap lead me to believe I was being stalked by the Devil. Stupid really, because the scariest thing I saw all evening was a slightly demented squirrel that scurried up an oak tree as soon as I got close enough to see it properly.

Stay calm, I kept telling myself, just stay calm!

It was when I was approaching the front door that I remembered my big mistake!

'Oh shit!' I yelled and listened as my words echoed through the alley. 'Triple shit!'

I couldn't believe how stupid I had been. I'd been so wrapped up in watching a tearful Abby fleeing from the house that I had completely forgotten to go back in and pick up the piece of paper I'd planted. I stared at my watch. Quarter past seven. My dad usually got home at half-past so it wasn't too late.

I legged it back up the side alley and sprinted along the main road. I ignored the rowdy boys across the street that were shouting things like 'Hurry up, you don't wanna be late now do ya' in stupid accents. I had to get back, preferably before my legs turned to mush and collapsed, which by my calculations would be in about five minutes time.

Patrick's words revolved in my head. 'Just because she loves him in a different way doesn't mean *she* won't hate being without him just as much as you do, maybe even more.'

Maybe even more . . .

Though there was nothing I could do about that now, except remove the evidence. If I didn't get there in time, I'd be on the next plane to Fiji.

I looked to the blackened sky as I ran full speed ahead. Clouds were forming above, covering the lit-up dots of the stars. I could tell I was about to be caught in a downpour. Why was everything turning belly up?

There was a clap of thunder and then my nose was tapped by a rain drop. I didn't stop running, no matter how much my legs cried out for a rest.

I found myself listening to the melody of the rain as it fell to the ground and then exploded around my pounding feet.

I couldn't see Dad's car outside the house. There was still time. My heart leapt three feet in the air and then slowed the pace of it's thumping down to be almost normal. I skidded on the soggy pavement as I ran round the corner. There was the front door. I pulled the key from my jacket pocket and slid it in the lock. My heart thumped against my ribs as the door opened – without my help!

'Millie!' my dad said, smiling. 'What are you doing here?'

'Umm . . . I left some important notes by the phone which I umm . . . need to pick up!'

Judging by the monster grin on his face, I could safely say that he:

a) hadn't noticed Abby had gone, and

b) hadn't seen the note.

'Do you want me to get it for you?'

'No!' I yelled. Dad gave me a puzzled look. 'It'll be easier if I do it!'

He shrugged and headed out the door. 'I'll be off now, OK? I can trust you to lock up?'

I nodded and asked, 'So, where's your car?'

'Round the back!' And he disappeared into the night.

Phew! Close one! I thought to myself as I scooped the piece of paper into my right hand. Really close one!

At home Mum was brewing up a storm.

'Where the hell were you?'

'Nowhere!'

'Who were you with?'

'No one!'

'What were you doing?'

'Nothing!'

'Right then, young lady! I can see I'm going to have to ground you!'

'But Mum, I haven't done anything!' I protested. I should've known better, Mum never gives up an argument.

'I trusted you to walk home by yourself. That was obviously a stupid thing to do, wasn't it! Let me guess, Megan needed help with her homework too?'

'Mum, come on, be reasonable!'

'Millie, I *am* being reasonable! I've always been too soft on you! You're grounded and that's final. From now on things are going to change around here!'

I gulped, I certainly didn't like the sound of that!

I stormed up the stairs passing a mad older sister in hysterics.

'Ha! Ha! Ha! Ha!' Rachel laughed. 'In your face!'

I stuck my tongue out at her rudely and then locked myself in my room. It was so unfair! Rachel had been snooping around with her boyfriend Nick for ages. She'd even ridden his motorbike a couple of times! I'd only slipped out of a party for twenty minutes or so and then wandered off on my way home afterwards. God! What if she'd known the truth of my disappearance?

You know sometimes you get the feeling that the big man upstairs has temporarily lent you to the Devil? The safe world that you know and love – with the happy family and great food – has disappeared, to leave you with the total devastation, lies, deceit and loneliness of reality. That's where I was at that moment, in the hands of the unforgiving Devil himself. I found myself lying on my bed, face wedged into the pillow and emitting some sort of loud wheezing noise, a true sign that things hadn't gone about in the usual jolly manner.

After some serious thinking (and devouring the contents of a chocolate box), I was feeling marginally better (but more than marginally wider). I didn't even realise the phone was ringing, so I was shocked to find myself picking up the receiver and muttering, 'Hello?'

There was a series of loud snorts, hiccups and sobs from the other end.

'Holly, what's the matter?' I sighed, trying to be sympathetic. I wasn't feeling like helping anyone at this moment. I just wanted to wallow in my own misery.

'Millie . . . it's . . . it's . . . me!'

'Oh my God! Dad, what's happened?'

I'd never been more shocked, surprised or struck dumb in my entire life. My dad, crying! And it was all *my* fault!

'She's gone!' he yelled, in between sniffles.

'Who's gone?' I said, trying my best to sound oblivious to his dilemma.

'Abby! I came . . . home ten minutes ago . . . and all . . . her bags were gone. Everything! What did I do, Millie? Why did she leave?'

I had to put the phone down then, mainly because at that moment, just before the word 'Millie', a surge of unbelievable pain had penetrated my body, paralysing me from head to foot. Let's call it guilt! I'd never heard my dad cry before. I always thought he was invincible, but hearing him like that just made me want to find a box of Kleenex and weep.

It's horrible enough witnessing an adult drowning in a lake of tears without knowing you're undoubtedly responsible for their pain. Not only had I hurt Abby, I'd hurt my dad too, the one person that this plan wasn't supposed to hurt. He was supposed to be himself again. He was supposed to just be back to normal. I guess I just hadn't thought of everything.

I pulled my duvet over me and prepared myself for an early night. After all, ruining two people's lives in one evening takes a lot out of you.

Chapter 16

X is for Xercising my intellect

'And the final goal, whoa, it was so completely amazing, you should have seen it!'

I brought my hand to my mouth and let off a horrendous yawn. I wasn't really in the mood for talking about football, I can't say I really cared who scored the winning goal. Did it matter who'd won? If Liverpool had won, bully for them, but what impact would the latest football scores have on my life? Just about as much impact as eating marshmallows for breakfast. But at least he seemed to have forgiven me for our little argument . . .

'But the ref was blind, I tell you! The amount of times he let Newcastle off for fouling, it was ridiculous.'

'Patrick! Look, I don't really care, OK?'

He didn't even seem to mind that much, he just continued to smile and silently mutter to himself.

It was an OK morning, it would have been a great one if I hadn't been feeling so rotten about Dad and Abby. It was a bit cold, but hey, it was November now.

The rising sun was popping its head out from behind a fluffy white cloud. Plus, the air was soooo fresh and it smelt like one of the deodorising sprays – you know – 'morning fresh', or something.

Patrick turned to face me and said slowly, 'Look, I hope you don't mind, but I told Justin and Solo we were going out!'

'You what?' I said, stopping dead in my tracks. 'I can't believe you!'

'Why?'

'Didn't we agree not to tell anyone? Are you completely deaf?'

'I don't see what the big deal is, Mill. So what if people know we're going out? Why should we keep it a secret?'

I glared at him. 'Because it's no one else's business, that's why!'

'What's up with you, Mill? I mean, I'd shout it from the rooftops. Why are you trying to keep it a secret? You're not embarrassed of me, are you?'

I stared at his face, that sweet smile, his cute little freckles. I loved him to pieces so why should I care what everyone else might say? I knew he wasn't handsome, even he knew he wasn't handsome, but why should that matter? I hadn't had a problem hanging out with him before. Why should this be any different?

I smiled at him and spread my arms out to give him one massive hug. 'Of course I'm not embarrassed of you!'

And we kissed, right in the middle of the street, and to tell you the truth, I didn't mind one bit!

'Good!' he said, grinning as we headed up the almost deserted road on our way to another day at predictable school. 'I guess it doesn't matter who knows, then!'

I sighed slowly to myself and brushed the wisp of hair that was obstructing my view aside. I held the brown curl for a second and gazed at it, the way all the hair folded together to form a soft spiral.

'What *are* you doing?' Patrick asked with a puzzled smile.

I let go of the hair and grinned back. 'Nothing whatsoever!'

Umm . . . now, I thought to myself as I surveyed the scene in front of me. How was I going to tell my mates about Patrick? I *did* have to, before word got around and they ended up hearing it off someone in the corridor and then telling me what a crappy friend I was for not trusting them. I was sure Jade would be cool with it, and Kaori. Megan wouldn't say anything. It was Holly and Lucinda I was concerned about. Well, Holly mainly. I was her best girl friend. What if she thought I was leaving her?

'Hey guys! What are you talking about?' I smiled at the girls who appeared to be deep in conversation.

Holly was trying to explain something to Lucinda, who wasn't paying a blind bit of notice to her. She seemed to be more interested in staring at the tall blond guy over Holly's shoulder. Jade, Megan and Kaori seemed to be chatting about something hugely secret because as soon as they saw me approaching they shut their gobs.

'We aren't talking about anything, Millie! Nothing at all!' Jade replied, smiling.

'Yep, we aren't talking about a thing,' said Kaori, grinning innocently, then she quickly added, 'especially not you!'

Jade rolled her eyes and gave a Kaori a light thump on her new pink jumper. 'Idiot!'

'What?' Kaori yelled as she rubbed the targeted area and then looked at Jade's stern face in disgust. 'What *is* your problem? It's not like I told her we were talking about her.'

Jade hit her again. 'Double idiot!'

I was tempted to giggle, I was *more* than tempted to giggle, but I casually stopped myself. After all, they had been chatting about me.

'So, why were you talking about me?'

Megan turned around and twiddled her fingers. Kaori looked at me and shrugged. Jade sighed loudly.

'Well?' I muttered impatiently.

'It's just that there's this rumour going around that you're going out with someone called . . .' She hesitated a moment. '. . . called . . . Patrice. Is it true?'

I gazed at my super silly, truly gullible and one hundred and fifty per cent delusional friend Jade, followed by the serious expression on mini-Megs's face and then Kaori's sneaky 'please tell all' nose wrinkle. Then I burst out laughing like a hyena with hiccups (and very bad hiccups at that). I glanced at Patrick, who was standing beside me, clutching his side in an attempt to stop the stitch he was getting from the hysterics that were gripping him.

'What's the big joke?' Holly asked, twirling her golden blond hair around her black polished fingernails. 'Tell me!'

Holly and Lucinda moved towards us stealthily, each wearing the same puzzled expression.

'Well?' Kaori tutted impatiently as her black stiletto boots tapped on the gravel drive beneath them. 'Well?'

I took a deeper than deep breath and let the cool air travel through my body, then I turned to look at Patrick. I sighed to myself. Now's as good a time as any.

I took Patrick's sweaty hand and tried my best not to imagine where it'd been.

'I'm going out with . . . umm . . .' I nodded in Pat's direction, smiled at him and then at my mates, 'I'm going out with Patrick!'

'Oh, at bloody last!' Holly said, rolling her eyes.

'What?' I said, confused.

Everyone else looked at Holly in wonder and bemusement.

'You finally admit it!'

'You, you knew?'

'Of course I knew, Mill! You're my best friend, I

could see the way you looked at him, the way you laughed with him. The way you mentioned his name *all* the time. How could I not have noticed?'

I smiled and threw my arms around her neck. She smiled back at me.

All my other friends decided to come over and hug me. Before long I found myself in the middle of a crowd of people, squashed until I couldn't breathe.

'OK guys,' I gasped. 'Let me out!'

They dispersed and I tidied my hair.

'I think it's great you're going out!' Megan said, grinning. 'Hey, maybe you could double date with me and Jason!'

I forged a smile, pretending to find that a great idea. Like I would really want to spend my time with Jason when every time I looked at him I was reminded of Matt.

'Yeah,' Lucinda agreed. 'You can come out with me and Will.'

We gazed at her in complete shock. Since when had she had a boyfriend?

'Will?'

'Yeah, Jason's mate. We hooked up at the disco, don't you remember?'

I shrugged, of course I didn't remember. How is one meant to remember when one hasn't been told?

'Can I get you something, Dad?'

I heard a small sigh from the almost lifeless body in

front of me. He looked absolutely awful! He was sitting on the sofa in his dressing gown. He hadn't washed, dressed or gone anywhere since she'd left. It was depressing, it was horrible, it made me feel more guilty than I ever imagined possible.

'I don't mind making tea, what would you like? Beans on toast? Scrambled egg? A sandwich?'

'No, it's OK, Mill, I'm not that hungry.'

'But you haven't eaten much for days. You'll be ill, you have to eat something.'

But there was no reply. I gave up, I'd done my best, what more could I do?

Chapter 17

Y is for Yahoo!

'So, Mill, you got what you wanted. Are you happy she's gone, is it just as you imagined?'

I groaned at Patrick and muttered. 'It's awful.'

'What? You are a fickle girl, Mill. You've been plotting to get rid of her for weeks and now that you've done it, well, it's awful?'

'No. It's not awful.'

'So it's good?'

'No! It's way way way worse than awful! He's so depressed!'

'Did you expect him to be happy when the woman he loves gets up and leaves him without a reason?'

'No, well, I thought he's be fine with it and we could go and do father and daughter stuff together.'

'But you always used to hate it when your father made you do father and daughter stuff. You used to beg me to come up with valid excuses.'

'Yeah, well, it was nice. I just didn't know it then. I mean, he looks really awful, you can't even start to imagine how bad! It's killing him, Pat, and seeing him like that is killing me!'

'No, that's the guilt, Mill!'

I sighed and looked at him. He looked back and said, 'Well, what are you going to do? You can't just take back all that you did, can you?'

'There's only one thing I can do!' I said, taking a deep breath.

'And that is?'

'Put on a brave face and go and see Abby!'

'But how will you find her?'

'I know she's staying with her sister.'

'How?'

'Her sister kind of left a message on our answering machine.'

Patrick stared at my guilty face.

'You wiped it, didn't you?'

I nodded. 'Anyway, her sister lives in Bridgend so all we have to do –'

'Hang on a second!' Patrick interrupted. 'Rewind there! Did you just say "we"?'

I nodded.

'No, Millie! No! No! No way! Absolutely not!'

'Why am I doing this, Millie?'

I looked at him, his solemn face rocking up and down on the bus.

'Look, you don't have to come in or anything. I promise, OK? I just need you here for, umm . . . emotional support.'

'Couldn't you have picked someone else? I'm not much good at emotional support.'

'No, it had to be you.'

'Why?'

I brought his face to my lips and kissed him.

'That's why!'

After an hour on the bus we arrived and jumped off, and began the search for Abby's sister's house. It wasn't hard to find, after we'd been down just about every turning at least twice. Eventually we discovered a small side passage which led to a main road. It wasn't long before we were ratter-tat-tatting on the red front door.

'Oh.' That was Abby's reaction when she saw two children, one familiar and one not so familiar, standing on the doorstep. Not 'Go away this instant' or 'Leave me alone, for crying out loud'. Just, 'Oh.'

I stared at her long and hard. Was there a real human being in there after all? I gazed at her small pale nose, her sky-blue eyes, her Barbie-blond hair. I couldn't tell, maybe there was more to Abby than met the eye.

I don't know, I can't explain it, but now I could see her for who she really was. Before, she seemed to be an evil being, someone who was taking my dad away from me, but now, now I felt, well . . . I felt was almost starting to like her.

She had certainly put on a bit of weight. Well, it

appeared that way. It wasn't much, maybe it had been there before, but I'd never noticed. I mean, I'd never looked at her properly. It's just it seemed as though the pink T-shirt she was wearing no longer hung loose, but hugged her stomach.

'Look . . .' I stuttered. 'You . . . you . . .'

I was finding it hard to get the words out. After all, asking her to come back was admitting I'd been wrong, it was accepting her as . . . as . . . as my stepmother! It was a big deal! No, a bigger than big deal! I hate admitting I'm wrong. What if simply asking her to come back wasn't enough?

'You . . . you have to come back!'

She looked at me as if I was speaking a foreign language, but the way her eyes communicated to me was unreal. I just watched them, moving back and forth as she shook her head.

'Please, Abby! He's a mess without you! He's like . . . like . . . well, a zombie!'

She raised her eyebrows slightly and without saying a word, beckoned us inside. I wasn't sure if Patrick was going to come in, but he did. He followed me inside like a lost dog. I was glad he did, he made me feel less nervous.

We sat down on the red leather sofa, just perched on the end of it, shuffling uncomfortably.

'Look, please come back!'

'Camilla, sorry, Millie, there is no way I'm going back in that house, absolutely no way! Not after being taken for such a mug. Did you know he was seeing someone else?'

I shifted myself slightly, this was going to be a great deal harder than I had anticipated.

'He's definitely *not* seeing someone else. He's crazy about you. Why else would he be so upset about you leaving?'

'Because he got found out, that's why! Lots of men have affairs, they just hate it when they get caught out. They've lost the game!'

'But my dad's not one of those men!'

'I used to think so too! Though now I know the truth. Men are all the same, liars, schemers and lowlife cheats!'

I watched Patrick twiddle his thumbs uncomfortably in the corner. His eyes were fixed firmly to the rose-coloured carpet beneath his dirty trainers.

'But Dad's definitely not seeing anyone!'

'Millie, you are so naïve! I've seen the evidence myself! There's nothing you could possibly say to get me within a kilometre of that man. You might as well leave now!'

Patrick stood up, shrugged and headed to the door quick as anything. I cursed his existence on the planet. He was supposed to help me. He was supposed to tell me what the hell I should do next.

'Stop!' I almost shouted. 'It's . . . it's all my fault!'

Abby looked at me, intrigued. Patrick was sliding his hand across his neck as if to say, 'Shut up right now.' He knew as well as I did that admitting the truth would get me in deep trouble.

'I . . . I . . . I pretended Dad was seeing someone else to get rid of you!'

Patrick mouthed 'no' as Abby's hands slipped their way on to her hips. I shut my eyes, wishing the whole scene would just disappear and I'd be home, Mum and Dad smiling at me, back together as if nothing had happened. Abby's voice shattered the moment.

'You . . . did . . . what?'

It was calmer than I had expected, I had been prepared for a full yelling, screaming, giddy fit.

'I set it all up . . . I wrote the message by the phone, it was me. I only wanted my dad back the way he was before. Though now he's worse than ever and you're the only person who can put it right again!'

There was more than a moments silence as Abby's eyes filled up with salty tears.

'I'm so sorry Abby, really, I am!'

'I'm just so relieved!'

My mouth opened so wide then, it could have been mistaken for a train tunnel. She was *relieved*?

'Well, I think I knew deep down that he wouldn't do anything of the sort.'

She smiled at me, nicely and that was when my hatred for her disappeared for good. I could see how much she loved my dad and how much he loved her.

174

They should be together. What right did I have to split them up?

'So, will you come back, then?'

Abby thought for a moment, and then grinned a diamond grin. I knew her answer before she even spoke it, her grinning white teeth said it all.

'Yes,' she announced. 'But what shall we tell your father?'

'Don't worry, I'll tell him everything.'

She smiled. 'I guess I'm coming back, then.'

Chapter 18

Z is for Zero problem

'Good luck,' Patrick said, smiling at me.
I smiled back. 'Yeah, I might need it.'

'It'll be fine.'

I sighed. 'I hope so.'

'He's got to give you credit for coming clean, right?'

'I guess.'

'Call me later, tell me everything.'

'How could I not?'

Once Patrick had disappeared into the house next door, Abby took his place beside me.

After she'd decided she was coming back, she packed up all her belongings and drove me and Patrick home. Now Patrick was gone and I was ready to face my dad. Out of the frying pan . . . into the fire.

'You ready for this, then?' she asked.

My eyes darted to the house and back to her. 'Ready as I'll ever be.'

So I picked up one of Abby's large bags and we walked up the path to the door.

I tried to picture the look on Dad's face as we entered, both of us, together. He'd be so confused, would he be happy to see Abby? Of course he would be. Would he be happy to see me?

I had no idea what I was going to say, I couldn't think of anything. How could he understand what I had felt? He wouldn't understand my reasons for doing it, though maybe he would. I had no idea how it was going to turn out. I just hoped I'd be alive at the end of it.

'Dad?' I called as I opened the door. 'Dad, you there?'

'Yeah, I'm here,' I heard him call from the living room.

I led Abby through the hall and hovered outside the room for a moment, peering round the door frame to see where he was. I couldn't see him. I didn't know if I was ready or not. It didn't matter, I was going in.

The knot in my stomach tightened as I walked round.

'I've brought someone to see you.'

I saw him before Abby entered the room, sitting on the sofa, blank expression, almost completely unaware of anything going on around him.

That was until Abby came in.

He sat up immediately and looked as though he was searching every space of his mind for something to say. He obviously failed because he just sat there, back straight, face full of confusion and he said nothing.

'Hi,' Abby said.

My dad just stared at her for a few moments more until finally coming out with, 'Hi.'

'Dad, Abby's come back to stay, is that all right?'

There were a few dazed nods from my dad's head.

Should I start explaining now? When Abby was there? Or was I supposed to do it on my own? Anyway, how could I talk to him when all he seemed to be capable of doing was staring at Abby?

'I'll go and unpack my stuff, shall I?' I heard Abby suggest from behind.

Dad was off the sofa in a flash.

'I'll help.'

'No,' Abby said, looking at me and smiling. 'Stay here, Millie has something she needs to say, don't you, Mill?'

I nodded slowly.

In a second, Abby was stumbling up the stairs with her bags and I was left with the moment, left with the moment I'd been waiting for, with the moment I'd been dreading. Here it was . . .

Dad stood in front of me, waiting for whatever it was I was going to say. But what did I want to say? Where did this conversation have to go?

'See, the thing is, Dad, I went to talk to Abby to get her to come back . . . '

'How did you know where she was? Why did you . . . when?'

'Let me finish, Dad. OK?'

He nodded carefully, wandered back over to the sofa and sat on it, creating a crease in the leather.

I hesitated for a moment, thinking how to start and then, then I told him everything. How I'd felt like Abby was taking him away from me, because he never had time for me any more. How jealous I was of her for always getting to be with him. How awful it made me feel when he cancelled our arrangements and how I decided the only way was to get rid of the woman he loved so much.

He didn't say a word as I explained how I'd tried to be horrible and sulky towards her, how I'd talked about Mum at dinner and how I'd looked through her things and found the photograph.

He didn't open his mouth for a second as I told him how annoyed I'd been when Abby was away and he decided he'd catch up on his paperwork and how I'd seen the building work at Abby's house as a perfect opportunity.

He listened as I told him all about searching Abby's house and then taking the key so the builders couldn't get in. He listened as I said how horrible it was of me and how awful I felt, and he listened as I told him about showing him the photograph.

His silence continued as I explained about the plan to make it seem like he was seeing someone else, to make Abby believe there was another woman in his life. I told him how I'd dabbed perfume on his coat and how guilty I'd felt afterwards. I explained how I'd called the house from a payphone and then hung up when Abby answered. Then I told him about the final plan, the note by the phone and how I'd left it there so Abby would have to see it.

I was fighting back the tears as I confessed to ruining both his and Abby's lives, as I confessed to watching Abby leave the house in a flood of tears I knew I was responsible for. I poured my heart out, telling him how awful it was for me to do that and how horrible I felt about the whole thing. I told him about deleting the answerphone message Abby's sister had left telling Dad where Abby was and I said that I felt so awful seeing how much of a bad state he was in that I had to take the bus up to Abby's sister to convince her to come back.

Eventually I found myself back in the present, eyes wet from tears, vision clouded with water so I could just see my dad's shocked face. He still said nothing, he left me to cry for a moment, he left the speechless air as it was.

I watched him as he lifted himself from the sofa and approached me, walking across the room step by step.

I waited for the uproar, I waited for the shouting. I got none of it.

Dad reached his arms out and gave me the biggest hug in the world.

'Oh, Millie,' he said above my sobbing. 'Millie, Millie, Millie . . . It's not all your fault. Sure, it was a stupid, horrible and deceitful thing to do, but . . . Well

. . . it must have been a shock. I should have eased you into it instead of pushing you into the deep end. I'm sorry about that . . .'

'I'm so sorry, Dad. I didn't know what I was doing, I didn't mean for you to be so sad. I'm so, so sorry,' I cried.

'I know, I know, I can see that, Mill.'

He wiped the tears from my face with a tissue he'd pulled out from his shirt pocket. Then he smiled at me.

'We'll talk more later. I'm going upstairs to talk to Abby.'

Epilogue – All's well that ends well

'So, did you . . . you know . . . kiss?' Jade giggles, going red in the face.

Kaori nods.

'Well . . .' prompts Lucinda. 'Details, please!"

'It was sooo romantic! Really gentle and there was this all over tingly feeling. It was . . . well . . . really amazing!'

'Tongues?' Holly asks.

There's more goofy nodding from Kaori. This sets all the other girls chuckling wildly, but to tell you the truth, I'm not sure that getting back together with Danny is the wisest decision Kaori can make. After all, it's still blatantly obvious that he hasn't changed a bit. He's a player and we all know he'll cheat on her again, I think deep down that Kaori knows it too. Though, you can't help who you fall for, can you? I know this first hand.

'Pass the Wine Gums, Mill!'

I chuck the packet in Megan's direction and she yelps as they hit her on the head.

'Sorry!'

The girls are all over at mine for the night, playing Truth or Dare. Big mistake! They've already eaten four packets of sweets, broken two of the attic floorboards and smashed a flowerpot (getting soil everywhere). It's only eight o'clock!

So, we're lying on the mattress, giggling at Kaori's answer to her Truth. 'What's the biggest secret that we don't know yet?'

I know, very original!

It's been quite a boring game, mainly because no one is being remotely daring. Everyone has gone for the soft option.

Now, humm . . . what's Megan going to pick?

'Truth!'

Oh God! What a shock!

'How many times have you snogged Jason?'

We watch as Megan's wine gum-filled cheeks turn tomato-red.

'Umm . . . about a million!'

We all burst out laughing again and listen to the echo it makes around the room.

'Millie! Can you be quieter please? You'll wake Leah!' Dad calls from downstairs in his 'I'm about to become very angry' voice.

'Keep it down guys!'

Yeah, it all worked out OK in the end. Dad and Abby have been back together almost a year now and I certainly don't mind. It's still unmistakeably gross when they're all loved up, kissing everywhere, but somehow, I survive. It's the price to pay for what I did and I get on OK with Abby now. She's actually, well, kind of nice. We go shopping together and out to the cinema, watch films while scoffing ourselves with Ben and Jerry's ice cream.

Patrick and I are still going strong – it feels like a match made in heaven. I can trust him with my life, he's always there for me when I need him (and when I don't) and there's nothing he wouldn't do for me. Surprisingly enough, Megan's still with Jason, even though my first impressions of him weren't exactly, well, very nice. You see, he's actually quite an OK guy. Kaori's back with Danny for the fourth time (when is she going to get it?) and Jade has started going out with, well . . . Patrick's mate Justin, of all people. It's funny how things work out, isn't it?

Oh yeah, the biggest news of all. All that time ago, when I went round to Abby's sister's to grovel and I thought Abby had put on weight. Well, she had, and now there's Leah, my three-month-old adorable baby sister!

If you would like more information about
books available from Piccadilly Press and how
to order them, please contact us at:

Piccadilly Press Ltd.
5 Castle Road
London
NW1 8PR

Tel: 020 7267 4492
Fax: 020 7267 4493

Feel free to visit our website at
www.piccadillypress.co.uk